I should like to thank Paul Ashley, Ronan Breen,
Erin Cole, Kath and Stan Fletcher, Eddie Holbrook,
Ian Prince and Chandrakant Patel for their help with
my research.

Orchard Books
338 Euston Road
London NW1 3BH

Orchard Books Australia
Hachette Children's Books
Level 17/207 Kent Street
Sydney, NSW 2000

A paperback original

First published in Great Britain in 2005
This edition published in 2008
Text copyright © Bernard Ashley 2005

ISBN 978 1 84616 957 1

A CIP catalogue record for this book is available from the British Library

1 3 5 7 9 10 8 6 4 2

Printed in Great Britain

The paper and board used in this paperback are natural recyclable products
made from wood grown in sustainable forests. The manufacturing processes
conform to the environmental regulations of the country of origin.

Orchard Books is a division of Hachette Children's Books,
an Hachette Livre UK company.

www.hachettelivre.co.uk

a BEN MADDOX
assignment

TEN DAYS
TO ZERO

BERNARD ASHLEY

ORCHARD BOOKS

TOP FLAT
130 LEYTON HIGH STREET
LONDON E10

BEN MADDOX to KATH LEWIS Producer World View Zephon
Television

URGENT – ASSIGNMENT ZT/OW/12/8

Kath

You gave me the assignment – here's the story supported
by solid sources. The file you're holding is photocopied
but I have the originals where they're safe, and everything
can be verified. I'm working on the script right now.

I hope you'll want to go ahead and slot this into the
schedule a.s.a.p., but because we don't want anyone 'got
at' before it's aired – I suggest we keep advance details to
a minimum, and only on the day.

But go for it! For the people of Magayana everyone here
has <u>got </u>to know. Also for the special female involved.

Just let the network know that this is going to be dynamite!

Ben

CONFIDENTIAL FILE

SECRET

Visit of HRH The Princess Royal to
Kensington Girls' High School

Tuesday, 15th October, 19.30

Security arrangements

Overview

Refer to previous briefing by Bodyguard DCI dated 30th September following preliminary visit to school.

15th October: HRH to travel by car from Gatcombe Park with detective (to be assigned when leave pattern determined), journey time 63 minutes, no outrider but preferential traffic lights on the A40 from 18.00 to be requested (liaison traffic division, New Scotland Yard, Inspector P. Lee). <u>She likes to drive herself – fast – be aware.</u>

Local police (Kensington Police Station) to provide external security at the school from 15.00 – liaison Chief Inspector Fallby.

School ticketing arrangements to be vetted by CID (DI Donaldson, Kensington Police Station) but approved by this office, Chief Inspector Paterson (Kensington) over-all i/c. <u>HRH doesn't suffer 'nutters' gladly.</u>

Press access – level 4 security, local, poss. national (arts)
Questions to HRH to be restricted to the business of the visit.

Timetable
12.00 School closes for half day
12.30 Sniffer dogs (local dog section) and visual sweep – liaise with Anti-Terrorist Squad, New Scotland Yard – DCI Trevor Shepherd
13.30 School declared and to remain sanitised, entry by authorised pass and invitation ticket only
16.30 Street barrier erected and policed, Lippard Street SW1, low profile
18.27 HRH leaves Gatcombe Park
19.00 Approved visitor list admitted to school building, Lippard Street entrance
19.15 Local Education Authority party arrives (5 persons, names to be submitted)

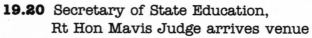

19.20 Secretary of State Education, Rt Hon Mavis Judge arrives venue

19.23 Secretary of State, Arts, Rt Hon Jim Dilly arrives venue
<u>Everyone except VIPs to be seated before HRH arrives</u>

19.30 HRH arrives venue, Lippard Street entrance VIP line-up to greet.

19.45 Performance by pupils and official opening of drama block by HRH.
<u>Check script for swear words and suitability two days beforehand.</u>

20.30 Presentation of school pupils and staff to HRH and government ministers, LEA party etc. according to submitted list.
<u>No gate-crashers. Pupils to be made aware of etiquette and royal protocol by school staff.</u>

21.15 HRH leaves venue, Lippard Street entrance for film premiere, Leicester Square, see separate briefing

22.00 Stand down

NB Some school pupils and staff concerned with performance will remain in building (Drama Block only) from 12.00 on the day. No access to other sanitised areas. Those leaving building will need passes to return.

<u>HRH is this squad's top level responsibility but all officers to be aware of anti-government feeling in some quarters – ref. the attendance of government ministers.</u>

CONFIDENTIAL FILE

Fran Scott – her story 1
(transcribed from tape)

Hello? Hope you can hear me because I'm keeping my voice down. This is Fran Scott. Frances Claire Scott. It's hard recording this, but it might be useful to someone, sometime. And I'm starting at the beginning – where else since I've got the time?

OK, from the 'off', Williams is a bitch – a right old bitch, and she can know it! She hears what I say to Gussie in the English lesson – a completely private conversation about not wanting to curtsey to Princess Anne – and she goes for me. There's no need for that, is there? Except she wants to make her point in case there's a general 'let's not curtsey to the Princess Royal' revolt on the night. Let's just keep it to stroppy me!

And I'm not helped by Gussie muttering next to me, 'Tell her, tell her – you reckon it, stand up for it!' – coming over all 'Black History' month.

I try telling Williams what I said was private but that's like telling a policeman you're only doing a private mugging.

'Nothing's private in my form room!' And old Williams can stare without blinking longer than any statue I've ever seen. All around me the others are fidgeting, slumping, yawning, throat clicking, all that stuff – and zipping up bags as loudly as they can because the bell's gone and they want away for half day. So I give it to her straight. 'I just said I'm not going to curtsey.'

'Then don't curtsey,' she jumps all over me. 'Stand there in the line and act sulky. Unless you'd rather not be there at all.'

She sits staring with her white powdered face looking like Elizabeth the First. And she's got Liz One's cunning, too, because she knows I'm definitely going to be there, having written the play we're doing – Gussie and me and the drama group. There was no way stinking Princess Anne coming to open the new drama block was going to keep me away, but it wasn't going to be easy, not curtseying, with Dad being Home Secretary.

Her Majesty's blooming Home Secretary.

Anne's mother's Home Secretary, if you think about it.

And what a good story that would be for the gutter press – **'HOME SECRETARY'S DAUGHTER SNUBS ANNE'** *– with ginger Mavis the Minister of Education, Dad's best enemy, looking on.*

'Your problem!' Williams says. 'You solve it – but you've got three more years in this school, remember that; class is dismissed.' All in one sentence as she goes out – that last threat said to me but meant for the others, like my father threatening to call out the troops to keep a picket line in order.

And what the others say as they race out I've blanked – like a lot of stuff I've blanked.

Well, by the time anyone hears this – if anyone ever hears this – you'll know why…

ZEPHON TELEVISION STUDIOS
– 'World View' – Leonard Wyatt to camera

Autocue
So the Magayana situation
remains unclear. Why isn't
the sugar cane being cut?
Why are the poor landowner
farmers in the north of the
country not being allowed to
export their crop?
The president claims he has
the support of his people in
letting the sugar rot, which
Claude Chaumet, the veteran
opposition leader in exile here,
would dispute. In his speeches
and articles, Chaumet hints
at secret activity going on but at
present is not responding
to our calls for an interview.
Meanwhile, as our film has
shown, there is much
unhappiness, poverty and
unrest back home, should
Chaumet ever decide – or dare –
to return there.

Len Wyatt was sweating in front of the cameras, straining to read his words from the autocue. Using his foot control, he held them where they were, but they seemed to be going away from him, getting too small for his staring eyes. He

11

just about got through to the end on memory and his knowledge of the story – before the studio manager signalled the cut and the red light on Camera One went out.

Ten seconds later the television journalist was on the studio floor, eyes wide open and mouth gasping for oxygen like a landed fish. And as the programme credits rolled, the station's doctor was pushing his way through the studio doors – but too late to do anything for the man who had all but died on camera.

In the control room every alert was flashing, especially on the face of Kath Lewis, the World View producer.

'Shit!' she said. 'Len's going to be the story – not Claude Chaumet!'

'Len's *died,* Kath!'

But Kath said nothing – and no one knew whether it was a hard heart or a soft spot for the man she'd never married that held her lips pressed tight together.

KENSINGTON W8

It's hard to get into a Knightsbridge pub with all the famous-name shopping bags piled on seats at lunchtime. But the caretaker at Kensington Girls' High School always had his favourite spot with a pint and a paper at a table for two in a quiet corner. Mostly he was alone, but with his year-round tan, close-cropped head of dark hair and the film star teeth, wearing an open necked white shirt and a well-pressed dark blue suit, occasionally a busy shopping woman would gratefully accept the offered spare seat, knee to knee.

All of which Laurina Modeste knew. Doug Way had been targeted for a fortnight.

On instructions from D, the leader of their team, he'd been followed by the man working with her – out of the school on his regular lunchtime break, as well as from his house in the school grounds on his evening outings on the Underground. And when his operational style had become obvious – the chat up, the offer of help with the bags, the calling a taxi after a second or third or fourth vodka and tonic, the occasional success and afternoon delight – they knew he was their target. A vain, over-sexed man, susceptible, and not too bright. If anyone would let them into Kensington High on a top security night, he would.

'You don't know me but I know you...' The well-built black girl with the wide eyes and fashion model nose and lips, slid into the seat opposite Doug Way. She looked like a pummelling masseuse but she sat daintily. 'My little sister's at your school.'

Doug looked across, took her in with a sip of his beer.

'What you drinkin', then?' Laurina Modeste lifted his glass to her own lips and tasted from it. 'Let me fetch you a refill of this.' Without waiting for a reply she went to the bar, came back with a new beer, sipped at it, and moistened her lips with her tongue. 'Take a taste of that. Tell us if I got this right...'

'Tastes fine to me.' The caretaker shifted in his seat.

'Mr Way, as you might tell, I've got a favour to ask.'

Doug Way looked into the big eyes. 'What's up? Your sister left something in the building? It's a half day Thursdays.'

'No, sir, it's a mite more than that. But we'd be grateful – so grateful you can't tell – if you could help us out. The two of us.'

'How's that, then?'

'I'm devastated. Dev-a-stated. You know Gussie Beckford?'

'Tennis player?'

'Kid in your school. Year Ten or Eleven, I never know which in this system here... I always reckon one good turn deserves another.' She flashed a promising smile.

'Know her face, I expect.'

'See, I'm her sister, come from the old country for a little visit, me an' her brother. An' what do we hear? She's performing in a play a couple of nights off, an' guess who can't get in to see her...?'

Doug Way regarded her over the top of his glass; he started to say something beginning with 'Tickets...' But a hand beneath the table was on his knee, a little squeeze...

'If you could wriggle us two in, I would be so grateful. So grateful. You want I give you some idea how grateful I would be...?'

But she was already doing so; and trying to keep his face straight, Doug Way told her how tight security was for a royal visit, why tickets had been strictly allocated weeks before the Princess's public engagements were known to anyone – but how he could always get a couple for himself. And against the clinking of glasses a date was fixed for a meet-up after the performance a couple of nights later, without Gussie and without the brother, of course. Gussie would be taken home by her mother while the two of them went off to heaven, following the departure of Princess Anne and the locking up.

A quarter of an hour later as the woman climbed into the taxi that Doug had called, she fished out her mobile and told her partner, 'Jesus forgive me for what I'm doing, but we've got him – an' got her!' She changed cabs three times on the way to the safe house at Battersea where, after talking to D on the phone, plans could be discussed for stage two of the mission – the kidnap of a special female.

ZEPHON TELEVISION

South Bank Studios – London SE1

INTERNAL MEMO

SIR REGINALD FEWSTER TO KATH LEWIS, PRODUCER WORLD VIEW

Further to the sad departure of Len Wyatt we have assigned recent trainee Ben Maddox to fill the vacancy in your team. Put him in where you see fit and move everyone up. CV attached. Maddox will report to you Friday next 12.00 for meeting prior to commence date following Monday 09.00.

RF

PS Don't judge him too quickly. Don't knock the rough go-get-'em edges off him. We could use some of that. RF

CURRICULUM VITAE

GENERAL
Name: Benjamin Russell Maddox
Address: Top Flat
                130 Leyton High Street
                London
                E10 19WW
Telephone: 020 8244 20131
Fax: 020 8244 25785
Mobile: 07808 720 2635
Email: b.maddox@a.net
Status: Single, non-smoker
Age: 24
Personal: 6', dark hair, hazel eyes

EDUCATION
Sherington School, Greenwich (primary)
John Roan School, Blackheath (secondary)
Sheffield Hallam University
Cardiff School of Journalism

QUALIFICATIONS
GCSE   Mathematics   A
                History   A
                Geography   A
                English Language   A*
                English Literature   B
                Science   B
                French   B
                Latin   C

A-Level	English Language	A
	English Literature	B
	Mathematics	A
	History	C

| AS-Level | Computing |

| BA Hons | Media Studies   First Class Honours |
| MA Journ | Journalism Studies |

EXPERIENCE

Holiday and vacation jobs as post office employee, hospital porter, milk and bread roundsman, casual assistant school caretaker, building site labourer, circus clown.

Work experience at Greenwich Mercury (local newspaper) as a reporter and at Meridian TV Studios (local TV news station) as a reporter and interviewer.
BBC Radio trainee reporter (8 months).
BBC London and South East local reporter (10 months) – trainee – non staff.

RELEVANT SKILLS

Professional journalistic – shorthand (100 w.p.m.) and typing (60 w.p.m.)
Sound recording, video recording, texting
Computer literate inc. website design
Clean driving licence – car and m/cycle

HOBBIES AND INTERESTS
Politics and current events:
Member of debating society at University
Avid newspaper reader (all titles inc. French)
Cinema: I have a keen interest in all new movie releases and enjoy all genres. Special interest in French and South American films.
Sport: I like watching most sports except baseball and play football and cricket. I am a good swimmer. Also juggler!
Music: Jazz and popular classics.

PERSONAL STATEMENT
I like digging out the truth and looking at it from all angles – I might have made a good detective but life in the police force wouldn't suit. I'm great on deadlines but poor on headlines, it's the small print, the watermarks that intrigue me.

Kath Lewis read the memo and Ben Maddox's attached CV. From her office on the ninth floor she could see out across the Thames, and with the sun shining on the City, the water reflected the new buildings imposed among the old London institutions. She thought again about the man who had died – and who she was privately mourning. What little slicker was this, coming to fill the gap in her team?

On its space age consul the television silently played the Zephon 24/7 news channel; it was never off. A Home Office spokesman was in the street outside his Department in Marsham Street being interviewed by a reporter. Kath clawed at the remote to punch up the sound.

'A decision about Claude Chaumet of the People's Democratic Party of Magayana will be made when we've taken evidence from the local police and the diplomatic service within the Foreign Office. If we deport him it will be in the light of knowing all the facts, and weighing all the options carefully.' He was stonewalling, he wasn't saying more. When pressed – more petted than pressed by a polite reporter – he would only repeat what he had just said.

'Len Wyatt would have got something out of him!' Kath reached for her almost empty glass of red wine. 'Had a way of knowing their weak spots...' She turned from the set and looked out of the window again. 'That's what we need in this business.'

BATTERSEA SW11

Up river to the west, in the Battersea flat, the two activists – Magayanan themselves – were watching the same news.

'They'll send Chaumet back 'less we pull this off, sure as

19

you get your hundred small ones to the dollar,' the man said: Augustin Baptiste, the male member of the hit team. Like Laurina Modeste, his female partner, he was fit and strong, belied by leanness and a slight stoop; his eyes stared with the intensity that anger and conviction give.

'But we're gonna pull this off, no?' the woman demanded. 'We're good as in, thanks to picking up some black girl's name and temptin' Mr Horny Caretaker. An' when we've got our target – well, won't they just jump to think again...' The woman's eyes were no less fired than her partner's at the audacity of D's plan. 'Jesus be praised, what a kidnap!'

Baptiste walked across the large sitting room to switch off the television set; or prowled, since whatever he did was on light feet. He turned, thinking, and flicked his fingers with a sudden agitated crack. 'Our man, Chaumet – he's got to be kept clean from all this, an' kept here to fight the battle. The man's our only chance.'

Laurina calmed him with the palm of a hand. 'That's the big point, no? Anyhow, he will be. Chaumet don't know about us, the Party don't know – not even most of our people don't know what we're doing. It's just D an' his people, an' us, an' the Lord Jesus. Stop frettin' on that, will you?'

Augustin Baptiste clicked in his throat. 'Then we got a white van to steal, plus buying locks an' chains an' food. An' three mattresses...'

'Yeah, don't forget the mattresses. We don't want her uncomfortable, someone as highly important as she is...' Laurina hitched herself in the doorway, big and beautiful. 'Or you could make one a double, man! You an' me, to keep the spirits up...'

Baptiste looked at her, just blinked once, slowly. 'We got this job to do, an' it could go to killing. People don't sleep cosy if they're goin' to kill.'

'I'm not talking about sleeping. I'm talking about taking your mind off things. It helps, don' it?'

Augustin Baptiste cracked his hand with a flick. 'Mattresses push together. If required.'

'Can do.'

'An' just as easy, they can come apart…'

At which Laurina frowned, before taking herself off to the kitchen.

LEYTON E10

In a kitchen in East London, Ben Maddox was tanking up on coffee. His girlfriend, Meera Sharma, had left for work at the publishing house, but propped up on the stainless steel work surface was a card she'd left – on one side a photograph of Bobby Moore lifting the 1966 World Cup in triumph, on the other the words Ben was reading, smiling.

Proud of you, Maddox! Top job. Now be top man at it. Go for Truth every time. And take no prisoners - they say Kath Lewis is a bitch.

Your loving girl
Meer
XXX

PS Hankies in top drawer, left. Only for show - use tissues.

Ben let the smile go and stared down into Leyton High Road with a serious, purposeful face – just to disguise his nervousness at going in to meet his new boss at Zephon News. He washed and dried his coffee mug, hung it up, and went to finish dressing, not forgetting a new white handkerchief from the Marks and Spencer pack in the top drawer, left. And no tissues. Top men in top jobs use a proper hankie if they want to.

CONFIDENTIAL FILE

Fran Scott – her story 2
(transcribed from tape)

So what's special about me? Other kids say I'm special, certain people say I'm special, but no one's special to themselves because they're them, aren't they? It's normal for me, natural, it's not special at all to have a dad who's the Home Secretary. It's not weird to me to have a policeman standing outside the front door sometimes, or a Protection Officer with us whenever Dad's moving about. And it's not special, it's dead normal, for Dad not to have a lot to do with us, what with his working breakfasts, briefings, working lunches, Cabinet meetings, tours of prisons and all that, speeches in Parliament, business dinners, and sleeping in his Westminster flat with his must-read files. Though he gives me a lift to school some mornings. He tries, but his job's normal to him, and it's normal to me. OK, I call the Prime Minister by his first name, the two-timing dog – but tons of kids have famous relations: actors and footballers and people in bands. They all get used to it. The same with Mum. 'Caitlin Jones' on the books and in the bookshop windows, writing her history books and winning her prizes, cooking dinner with a spoon in one hand and a pen in the other – living a life that's nothing special to me.

A lot more special than all that is having my little Mikey for a brother – the not sure boy who needs his Big Sis – and when he has one of his attacks I could be a nurse. And that's really special.

But this – what's going on, this isn't special, I tell you. No, not special at all.

I'm going to make a fool of myself, so switch off!

(tape clicks)

SOUTH BANK SE1

Kath Lewis spent her smiles like some people spend a thousand pounds. Carefully. They say that every living creature is allocated the same number of heartbeats before they die, on average. Gnats' hearts beat fast, elephants' beat slow, but there's the same allocation across all the species. Kath Lewis seemed to feel the same way about smiles – she acted as if everyone has been allocated so many, and she was going to live to be a hundred.

When Ben Maddox knocked and came straight into her office on the stroke of noon she was frowning at a transmission schedule on her desk. She scowled at the interruption – and then had to spend one of her smiles. She'd seen the new man's photograph but when she saw him in the flesh she knew immediately why Sir Reg had given him a television contract instead of radio. This boy was what television was all about: decent height, but not so tall that people being interviewed would be forever looking up; glossy dark hair, not fussy or making a statement; straight nose – no problem for a camera; and bluey-green eyes that shone without staring. Telegenic.

'Kath?'

'Kathleen Lewis.'

'Call you Kath?'

And a sexy voice. She nodded.

'Call me Ben.'

'Oh, I shall. When it isn't Shite-face Ben, or Cock-up Ben, or—'

'Wonderful Ben?'

'You've got it. Sit down.'

Ben sat; no fussing with trouser hitching or jacket flaps or leg crossings; just sat, like a polished actor, opposite her at the desk.

'I've read your CV.'

Ben nodded. Of course she had.

'And I've watched a training feature you did on London's homeless.'

'What did you think?'

'It was crap. The concept. All the male trainees do London's homeless, all the women do chorus girl to star. What really interests you?'

Ben was unruffled, and, rarely for her, Kath Lewis didn't flicker away to check what was happening on the ever-playing TV. 'Is that important in this job?' he asked. 'Shouldn't everything interest me – or nothing? I shouldn't be there as a person, as Ben Maddox, I should be there for the viewer, drawing out—'

Kath Lewis slapped her hand on the desk: a practised, loud slap. She had a special cleared space for it. 'Oh, don't give me that "conduit" rubbish! You'll talk about "enabling" next, or "accessible". If you've got no personality, if you don't come from somewhere, you're no good to a programme like ours.'

'You want attitude?'

'I *love* attitude, live for it. It's what Len Wyatt had. You knew where he was coming from although he never *told* you where he was coming from. When he had a politician on toast you knew he meant it although he never showed you he meant it. It just came through. He played the neutral game his own partisan way. People need to know you care.'

'Oh, I care, Kath.'

'Then don't give me job interview answers. Ever. You mention truth in your CV. What truths do you care about?

What current stories would you chase?' Now she took the first glance aside to the television set.

'Not the rubbish on that monitor right now.' Ben leant forward, but just a little. Had Kath Lewis been a camera she'd have had no need to re-focus on him. 'London Underground! There's no story about the London Underground that isn't told every night at half past six – when the only people who might be interested are still trying to get home on it. And how many people in Liverpool care about Transport for London?'

'Easy target. What, then?'

'I like stories that aren't stories; so-called truths that no one even suspects are lies. It's not the *undetected* crimes society needs to worry about, it's the *unsuspected* crimes.'

'Neat. Ish. Who told you that?'

'My brother. He works at Scotland Yard. One of the squads.'

'Which one? Flying, Vice, Fraud, Anti-terrorist…?'

'Can't say.'

'Protecting your source?'

'Protecting my arse.'

Kath Lewis topped up her red wine and sipped at it, no offer of a glass to Ben. 'So, you tell me – what's an unsuspected crime at the moment?'

Ben glanced round the big office, took in the shelves of labelled video boxes, pointed at one leaning last-guy-in-the-line on a level with their heads. 'Claude Chaumet,' he said, 'Magayana, what Leonard Wyatt was homing in on. Why deport an opposition leader whose work permit hasn't expired on so-called breaches of his residency conditions? For what, putting out his wheelie-bin late? What *is* going on out in Magayana to make our immigration people start acting like

Joseph Stalin, sending home to a dodgy fate those people who oppose their president?'

'What fate?'

'They'll hang him, for sure.'

He had hit a special spot, the story Len Wyatt had been working on with Kath Lewis. *Finger on the pulse, Maddox!*

'So, you'd want to get "on the road" out there, would you? Follow Wyatt? See what's going on in Magayana for yourself?'

'Wouldn't mind.'

'*Wouldn't mind?*' Kath Lewis nearly spat into her wine. 'That's nowhere near strong enough for a return flight to Magayana. *Wouldn't mind* wouldn't get you to Margate, Maddox!'

'OK, yes, Kath, I want to go.' And he let his eyes tell her how much.

'Our senior reporters are tied up with the PM and his personal problems, that scandal's the headline story, so why not let the new boy have a go?' She was asking the wine. 'Or the new girl, Bloom Ramsaran...?'

'Oh, the new boy. Definitely.'

Bloom Ramsaran had joined Zephon a couple of week before Ben, and all reporters are rivals.

Kath nearly smiled again. 'OK, I'll give it some thought – just you and Jonny Aaranovitch and a small camcorder. Like you do, like Len did, I think there's something going on out there that needs to be uncovered; a truth out there, and a lie to be laid bare here at home, close to the heart of government.'

Kath swept her arm round to take in Big Ben and the Westminster scene through the huge picture window – knocking the half glass of red wine over the displeasing schedule on her desk.

'Bugger!'

In a neat move, Ben was on his feet and mopping up the wine.

'Thank you, Ben.' And she spent another smile. 'Now just look at your nice white handkerchief!'

'I'll tell my girlfriend it's blood. She works for a publishing house.'

'You should have used a tissue.' Kath Lewis plucked a handful from the box on her desk.

'You're right,' Ben said. 'With hindsight.'

METROPOLITAN POLICE

MISSING/STOLEN VEHICLE

Telford Grove
Station no. 298

Vehicle   Make: Ford
            Model: Transit Van
            Colour: White
            Registration: N350RPD

Owner   Stephen Richard Samuels

Address   138 Hartley Avenue
            London E6 1QR

Tel no.   020 8534 85586

Mobile no.   07029896620

Details   Vehicle reported missing by owner at
07.00 hours Monday 14th October.
Last seen outside house 22.30 13th
October. Van locked and secure, alarm
set, no tools left in van.
Owner heard no sounds, no alarm.
Neighbours saw/heard nothing.

DVLS informed. Vehicle added to
missing lists 07.15 14th October.

'Mind this floor! I want no scuff marks on this new floor. The lovely lady's opening our drama block, not coming for a buff-up.'

Kenny Richards, head of theatre studies, was finishing the rehearsal. It had gone as well as could be expected, considering that things were at that stage where the funny bits and the shock moments weren't new any more – it would take an audience to bring that first *kepow*! back into all that. But most of the lines were solid and they'd all stopped bumping into each other on the moves.

Fran Scott and the group had researched a strong play about some women prisoners in Holloway who put on a show for charity. 'The show within the show'. Gussie did a sultry love song and Fran's character tried jealously to ruin it for her, ending with a stage fight to the music of 'I've Never Been in Love Before' – as carefully choreographed as a ballet. This was the end of Act One. Now, out of breath, eyes shining with having got the moves right and finishing in time to the music, Gussie ended up with Fran pinned to the floor.

'Right!' shouted Kenny Richards in his precise voice, as always acting up his own safe camp character for the girls at Kensington High. 'Upsadaisy, Gus. Lovely! But really arch that neck at the end: you're on top: I want the proud panther look, not the fagged-out bridegroom." He clapped his hands to kill the laugh. 'And now, ladies, in the break – curtsey time. Royal etiquette.' And he dropped a perfect curtsey himself, like Darcy Bussell at a Royal Command Performance. 'Let's get this right for Annie…'

He lined up the cast in presentation order and went down the line introducing himself as HRH to every member of the cast and crew, nodding regally to each girl. Gussie screwed her mouth to mutter something to Fran but Kenny Richards got his word in first. 'Yes, I know I'd make a lovely queen, Gus, so watch how it's done.' On he went down the line, each girl bobbing as he faced them. 'Ball of foot behind right ankle, slight bend of both knees, arms at the sides straight as an Irish dancer's. And up.'

There were variations. Some went lower than others, there were wobbles, but all in all the drama group were good movers.

'That's it, ladies, *act it.* Old-fashioned smarm. You can smile, but not a single word to HRH unless spoken to, and then a short polite reply. It says here. She doesn't need to know how you've sweated like pigs to get this right, and you don't need to know how her haemorrhoids are. Or the Queen's.'

By now he'd reached Fran, at the end of the line. 'And I'm told we've got a problem with you, Miss Voice of the Republic...' But his eyes were twinkling and Fran didn't feel threatened. 'A little bird tells me you don't want to curtsey.'

Fran nodded. 'That's right.'

'Not just a weeny millimetre...?'

She stared him out. 'It's not the millimetre,' she said, 'it's the milligram – of principle. It's in here.' She tapped her forehead. 'One human being should never be subservient to another.'

Kenny Richards sighed. 'So at the final black-out, Frances Scott, you run forward out of the set with the others, line up where you are now, and just drop off the end and go behind the curtain...'

'OK.'

'...and put the kettle on. Start the Coffee Republic.'

'Make mine a coca!' said Brigitte Vernay.

Fran nodded.

'Any questions?' Kenny Richards held his hands pressed together.

'Why have we got *her*?' Alice Sutton wanted to know. 'Why couldn't we have Prince William?'

'Why couldn't any of us, love? Because they're all allotted out, the jobs. It's how the Queen keeps order. Upset E. Regina and you get an afternoon opening a Sewage Recycling Plant. Keep her sweet and you get a night with us, followed by James Bond.'

'Will there be police and Special Branch?' Rose Petty wanted to know.

'Only token.' The teacher showed them his empty hands. 'Because who in the world would want to harm the Princess Royal?'

And on that there was general agreement; Anne was no way politically important enough to warrant mega security.

ZEPHON TELEVISION

Transcript for Legal Department

PROGRAMME: ZT/OW/12/8 41   **WORLD VIEW**
TRANSMISSION: TO BE DECIDED

BEN MADDOX INTERVIEWS – MAGAYANA

Ben Maddox (to camera, above the Presidential Palace):

Magellan, the capital of Magayana. Sunny, sultry,
tropical coastline to the south for rich tourists.
(Shots of Riga Beach, bronzed tourists on the fringes of the sea)
And to the north? Well, that's sunny, too – but sweaty,
and charred dirty with burnt sugar cane.
(Shots of muscular men cutting cane)
Hands are grimed with it, lungs choke on it. So
wouldn't it be good if these hard working people to the
north, enslaved by our sweet tooths, had some other,
cleaner natural resource to sell to the world?
*(The large bundles of cane are thrown into a steel barge in
a creek)*

Ben Maddox (to camera, against a line of burnt cane):

Well, perhaps they have. Under here. *(Stamps feet)*
Never mind the acres of sugar cane around me, enflamed
to remove the foliage. They've been told to forget all
that, and of course, they're wondering why.
*(Cut away establishing shot of Jesus Guimet walking along a row
of rotting sugar cane towards camera)* Jesus Guimet works –
or worked – a plantation here.
(To Jesus Guimet) So what is going on, what is under here?

Jesus Guimet (a tall, prematurely old 40-ish black Magayanan):

Nothing – is what they're telling us, huh! *(Flicks his hand)* There's nothing to worry our heads about. Like we're the poor, silly-black-boy natives who dance for a string of beads. Except we know they want to dig some stuff out, something that's under our sugar cane. And this is our birthright lands, we're freehold farmers, we own these fields. *(Shot of a wide sweep of big fields of sugar cane divided by waterways)*

Ben Maddox:

So where's the problem there? If this is your land, don't you own what's beneath it?

Jesus Guimet:

No, sir! You got a house?

Ben Maddox:

OK, yes, for the sake of argument.

Jesus Guimet:

You own it? It's yours?

Ben Maddox:

Let's say so.

Jesus Guimet:

In London? *(Cut-away shot of Ben Maddox nodding)* And you own that bit of the London Metro that runs underneath you? You own the sewers, the telephone cables, the magma, the core of the earth? You own the bit of

Australia directly under your house?

Ben Maddox :
No.

Jesus Guimet:
No more do we. No one does.

Ben Maddox :
So how deep do you own?
(Cut to a shot of a poor cluster of dwellings, mud walled and thatched with sugar cane foliage. A group of undernourished children sit in the shade staring at the camera without smiling. A mangy dog runs through the shot)

Jesus Guimet:
Six feet. Enough to get buried an' the dogs don't dig you up. And this stuff is deeper than that and it belongs to President Gomez. An' he's driving us out of our lands by putting a block on the paperwork for our sugar, just so they can come in and dig this stuff out, we reckon…

Ben Maddox:
(Voice over, in Magellan, interior of the Ministry of Trade, interviewing Manuel Coelho, against a shot of a bald, sixty-year old white man in a dark suit, sitting in a large armchair in front of a window view of the capital): I asked Manuel Coelho, the president's spokesman, what this mineral could be. *(Close-up of Coelho)* Thank you for seeing me. We're interested, sir, in what's happening in the north of your country.

Manuel Coelho

Mr Maddox, the President's got no secrets. You ask me what's happening in the north? Nothing. Absolutely nothing.

Ben Maddox:

Nothing? Really? Well, perhaps 'nothing' is right – because the sugar isn't being cultivated, is it? Nothing's happening to it – why is that? Why isn't the sugar crop being cut and exported?

Manuel Coelho:

(Smiling) Oh, there's no mystery there. There's a glut in the market. We're holding off.

Ben Maddox:

For a higher price?

Manuel Coelho:

That's the usual reason.

Ben Maddox:

But how do these people live, without selling their sugar? What else do they have?

Manuel Coelho:

What else we have, Mr Maddox, is a very good benefits system here – and next year these farmers will benefit hugely when the price goes up. We are doing them a big favour.

Ben Maddox :

This isn't because there's something under the ground, something you want to mine, is it? Gold, perhaps, or diamonds? That's the word...

Manuel Coelho:

(Smiles dismissively) The President's got no secrets. There's
nothing there. Someone finds a bit of something
semi-precious and word spreads that they're standing on a
fortune. We've looked – there's nothing significant.
Metamorphic rock can be very poor.

Ben Maddox:

Is this 'nothing' that is there, this 'nothing' to worry
about, exactly what Claude Chaumet is worried about,
what he's drumming up interest about – your Opposition
Leader exiled in London? He's looking for action against
you, isn't he?

Manuel Coelho:

I truly don't know what he's worried about.
(He leans forward smiling again, showing the gold in his teeth)
Just ghosts in the dark...

Ben Maddox:

Is it true that you want him back? Extradited from
Britain? Deported?

Manuel Coelho:

If he's got things to say then he needs to be saying them
here. Healthy debate is what the president likes.

Ben Maddox:

And he'd come to no harm if he returned?

Manuel Coelho:

Mr Maddox, that doesn't even deserve an answer.

Ben Maddox:

You still have the death penalty for treason?

Manuel Coelho:

Mr Chaumet knows that healthy democratic debate is not treason. And thank you for your interest. (He starts to get up)

Ben Maddox :

Is there a chance that I could talk to President Gomez?

Manuel Coelho:

(Reaching out to shake Ben Maddox's hand, bowing):
Thank you, Mr Maddox. *(He gets up and goes to the door)*

Ben Maddox:

Thank *you*, Mr Coelho.
(Cut)

Ben Maddox:

(Exterior, against the original view of the capital, Magellan): Is there something happening in the north? Why isn't the sugar harvest being cut and sold? *Are* people suffering? And what is the British connection? Why does President Jorge Gomez want Claude Chaumet brought back here, and why might the British government allow it? Many questions to which we have few answers.

This is Ben Maddox, 'World View', Magellan, Magayana.

BAYLIS AND FEWTRAL
HOUSE AGENTS, LETTING AGENTS

79 STAINES DRIVE, HOUNSLOW, MIDDX. TW4 8ER
TEL. 020 88594 8531

AGREEMENT between Messrs Baylis and Fewtral
and Richard Leonard Richmond of 36 Cheshire Street,
Battersea, London SW5 8ER for the short term rental
(six calendar months) of business storage premises at
36-38 Denby Avenue, Hounslow, Middx. TW4 7BD

AS SEEN and approved by the lessee

COMMENCING: 1st October next

MONTHLY rental payable in advance: £2,300

DEPOSIT: £1,000 by Visa 4839 7784 9321 7006

SERVICES: Gas non-inclusive
           Electricity non-inclusive
           Water rate inclusive

DEPOSIT received with thanks

REFERENCES returned herewith

FOR and on BEHALF of Baylis and Fewtral

F. J. Powell

KENSINGTON DRIVE W8

Ben Maddox knew where the Home Secretary lived and where he had his Westminster flat. Zephon Television had addresses, phone numbers, mobiles and e-mails for everyone in public life. A string of researchers kept the 'library' list up to date, together with everyone's diary engagements, their favourite restaurants, their clubs, and – when they were hot news – their whereabouts from minute to minute. And when Ben had received his letter of acceptance for the Cardiff School of Journalism he had started his own private files taken from newspapers, magazines, TV interviews. He could call up celebrities' quotes, favourite foods, drinks, drugs, girlfriends, boyfriends, children, anything that was innocent at the time but might be dynamite later; anything that might give him an edge or an 'in'. His brother in Scotland Yard helped, too. He dropped hints to Ben about personal stuff that CID knew, things that weren't protected by the Official Secrets Act and wouldn't compromise any operation, the way a detective might talk to his wife. Like, the name of the TV family comedian who was really in drug rehab while his agent's publicity said he was touring Australia, that sort of thing. And Ben was very discreet.

Now Ben was door-stepping the Home Secretary at his Kensington house. The Zephon team knew that he'd slept there overnight and not at his Westminster flat, and they knew that he had a nine-thirty meeting at the Home Office. They had asked for an interview there, but it had been refused; neither would he come to the studio or do *Today* or *Channel Four News*. So Ben Maddox took his sound cameraman Jonny and waited in the street to pounce.

The house was Georgian in a smart Kensington side street

– large porticos, wide front doors, shallow steps. Each house had a basement area from the days of 'below stairs' servants – and some still had domestic staff, but not next door to the Minister's. So that was where Ben and Jonny waited. The policeman on ministerial door duty saw them arrive and blanked them. He made no move to communicate with anyone inside – freedom of the press, and Jonny Aaranovitch was a known face – but they stayed out of his sightline in case he changed his mind.

Ben was ready, he'd done his homework. He knew that the Home Secretary, Dennis Scott, came from a well-off background, had one older sister to whom he rarely spoke, was an Oxford rugby blue, had got a lower second degree in English Literature, preferred Shakespeare to Sondheim, and had a weakness for young secretaries – although no one had ever caught him doing anything about it. His wife was a published historian and he had two children, Frances and Michael – but they came well down his list. He never spoke publicly about them, nor put 'family' among his relaxations. But Ben knew that unless he had a breakfast meeting or a *Today* interview, a car would pick him up from Kensington at eight o'clock, and that not only Dennis Scott but his daughter would come out, for a lift to school.

The government Rover drove up to the door at 08.00 precisely, a protection officer in the front passenger seat. Ben saw the duty policeman give the 'car arrived' signal back through the glazed front door, and out came the minister. And out from their basement stepped Ben Maddox and Jonny Aaranovitch, the camera running, sound and vision.

'Home Secretary, good morning, sir. Zephon Television, can you tell us what Britain's position is on Magayana? Why aren't they exporting sugar to us this year?'

The 'Prot' officer was out of the Rover with a protective arm and the Home Secretary was about to wave Maddox away, but Dennis Scott must have thought he had a better dismissal than that. 'That's Foreign Office,' he said, 'or Department of Trade. Wrong man!' He smiled smugly for the camera, turned back to the house with an arm out for the daughter who hadn't followed.

'Is Claude Chaumet the wrong man? Don't the government like him? As Home Secretary are you going to send him back to Magayana?'

Dennis Scott froze for just a second, then he beckoned impatiently behind him to the front door, one of those 'bloody-hurry-up!' gestures fit only for family. And out came Frances Scott, the daughter.

'Sorry, I might let you delay me,' the minister said, 'but my daughter mustn't be late for school. Be in touch with my office.' And he swept her, in Kensington Girls' High School sweatshirt, skirt, baseball cap and big sports bag, down the steps and into the back of the Rover.

'On what grounds will you make your Claude Chaumet decision?'

But Ben Maddox had had all he was going to get from the Home Secretary. He got the flat palm of the hand on the window saying 'no comment' as the car drove away.

Ben gave the 'cut' sign to Jonny. 'One nil to him,' he said. And they went to find some breakfast – croissants and several cups of strong coffee. People always need the help of something strong when explaining failure to the likes of Kath Lewis.

CLAUDE CHAUMET
PEOPLE'S DEMOCRATIC PARTY OF MAGAYANA
33 WESTCOMBE PARK DRIVE, LONDON SE3 8ER

`DRAFT - to be retyped`

Florence Cole
Secretary General
United Nations
Usual address
`To be dated`

Madam General Secretary

I have the honour to be the leader of the official Opposition Party to my country's government of Magayana. I am at present under house arrest and the `threat? / possibility?` exists of deportation to my homeland where my situation would be uncertain. However, my personal circumstances are not important.

At present my people's sugar harvest is being denied export by President Jorge Gomez and the government of Magayana. It is burnt but uncut and rotting. The excuse that this is an economic measure to push up prices is derisory. I am convinced that there are other reasons and they lie in the ground in the north of my country, beneath the sugar plantations. On behalf of the affected farmers of my country, and on behalf of the People's Democratic Party of Magayana I demand X `seek` under Human Rights a meeting with you to explore the possibility of a United Nations ruling lifting the embargo on the export of sugar from Magayana. I urge you to make your response with some urgency.

I have documentation to support my concerns.

Yours, etc. C.C.

Ben Maddox and Jonny Aaranovitch were in the Zephon TV Newsroom viewing the brush with Home Secretary Dennis Scott that morning – awaiting a stiffer brush with Kath Lewis.

'Nice pictures!' Ben said.

'Nice style! Not too yappy, the tone.'

Ben was pleased; Jonny worked with the best. 'But nothing for the news, let alone Kath. Taking the daughter to school. Nice ploy. Anyone coming on at him has got to sound churlish in front of the kid...'

But Jonny was shaking his older, balding head. 'Every day, he does this? Takes the daughter to school?'

'Some, diary permitting.'

'Not right.'

'I said, it's his ploy, a bit of protection...'

'Not right.' Jonny ran the frames on, stopped them again with the girl stepping out of the gate onto the pavement. 'Not right, she doesn't look.' He wrinkled his perceptive nose. 'Somehow. This going to school. What school is this?'

'Kensington Girls' High.'

'It's there – can't put my finger on it...'

Ben came over his shoulder to stare at Fran Scott in her school uniform – sweatshirt and cap with the KGHS interwoven badge on them. The sportsbag. No jewellery.

'That's the uniform, Jonny, sweatshirts and baseball caps. All that St Trinian's schoolgirl stuff – ties, blazers and white blouses – that's old hat now. This looks all right to me.'

'Pervs!'

Ben spun round at the voice; Jonny stayed looking at the frame, didn't move a muscle. It was Bloom Ramsaran, the Trinidadian girl who'd come to work at Zephon just before Ben.

'This is the Scott thing?' she asked.

'Yeah, I tried to—'

'I heard. You failed.'

'Can't win 'em all...'

'Aah.' Bloom patted Ben on the shoulder, held it there for a second. 'And here's me doing rubbishy girls' stuff about the new Bond film – but at least it's going out on the six o'clock...'

Ben turned at the contact but she walked off. He went back to the still frame.

'There's something, I tell you.' Jonny shrugged. 'This, we keep.'

'We keep what?' Kath Lewis came into the newsroom, weaved her way between desks of monitors and computers to Ben's corner, and stared at the still frame of Fran Scott. 'Is this what you got, the daughter?'

'He takes her to school. Saw me off, acted the diligent, loving parent.' Ben waited for Kath's rasping disappointment.

'Perhaps he's not acting,' she said. 'But you'll find that out, "door-stepping". You could surprise him a hundred times before you got under his waistcoat...'

'Yeah.'

'...but Zephon isn't that patient. Do better next time, eh?'

'Yes, ma'am.'

She went, and Ben turned to Jonny for at least a grin of sympathy. But the cameraman was too engrossed, still staring at the frame of Fran Scott that was puzzling him.

That evening, Ben read over his papers and notes as he sat in the small kitchen of their flat where Meera was stirring one of her famous Madras curries.

'Wine?' she asked him.

'I should've got something out of Scott this morning.' Ben stared on at the spiral notebook and the papers tucked into it. 'That man's on a knife edge, he's got that look.'

'Ben, I said, "wine?"' Meera sliced a cucumber like someone trained by Jamie Oliver.

'I am whining. I came over like a novice.'

'You are a novice.'

Ben went on flipping at his notebook with one hand as he pulled a bottle of Burgundy from the wine rack. 'Scott's political life's up in the air, I can just sniff that. See, he's got two choices: he does what I reckon the Prime Minister wants and deports Claude Chaumet, but he finds himself holding the dynamite stick of voters who care; or he proves himself a man of principle, refuses to do what the PM says – and gets the sack.'

'Spicy!' Meera slid two curries onto the kitchen table, took a jug of iced water from the fridge, and turned his papers round to look at them.

CAITLIN JONES

WELCOME TO MY WEBSITE

This isn't an all moving, singing and dancing website, it's self defence rather than vanity.

In answer to many requests for information about me and my books I have decided to condense a few facts here. All other queries should be directed to my publisher, Boadeccia Books, 108 Maiden Lane, London WC2X 8YR.

I was born and brought up in Hemingford Grey, Hunts., educated at St Ives Girls' Grammar School and Clare College, Cambridge.

Writing throughout my university life, I was first published by The Heffer Press in 1980 with a biography of Elizabeth Fry. I have since published ten biographies – all of women – and eight novels. A list follows.

My latest book is a novel, *Nelly Mabel Powell*, the story of a poor girl growing up at the turn of the last century, torn between her working class family's values and

the 'lady led' suffragette movement.
ISBN 1- 903015 – 28 – 6 – Z   £16.99 (hardback)

I am married with two children, living in London with
my politician husband, Dennis Scott, currently
Her Majesty's Home Secretary.

For me, writing is a way of life.
My order of priorities is family first and writing second
but my husband and children could be forgiven
for thinking it's the other way round!

Meera slid the paper round again and looked at Ben's notebook.

Notes on family of Dennis Scott, Home Secretary

Daughter: Frances Mary Scott, age 15+
Attending Kensington Girls' High School, Year 11
What subjects, interests, health, friends?

Son: Michael James Scott, age 11
Attending St John's CE Primary School, Year 6
Academic? What secondary school chosen?
Sporty? Health? Other interests?

Wife: See website.
Rarely appears with Dennis, she's her own woman.
Good mother? What's her next book?

'You're not stooping to using his kids, are you?' Meera demanded. 'That's tabloid gutter stuff!'

'And what...about the...kids in Magayana?' Ben's mouth was puffed like a blowfish on his first hot forkful of curry. 'There's no work for their parents while their own sugar cane rots; all they can do is apply for piss-poor benefit, while Jorge Gomez and his presidential lot are waiting to start mining whatever's under their own land.'

'Which still doesn't make this route ethical, Benjamin.'

Ben was starting to sweat. But he was fairly relaxed about having gone to an old Cardiff mate at the *Sun* and bought him a drink in exchange for the Scott family notes.

'I'd only use facts, not people. Anyhow, these politicians keep their kids well away from their jobs.' But as he spoke Ben Maddox was away in his own mind, remembering what Jonny Aaranovitch had said that morning about something not being right with the daughter, something not tying in. And when an old news dog like Jonny squinted his eye, there was usually something to see...

'Mmm,' he said, remembering to fork again. 'Delicious.'

CONFIDENTIAL FILE

SECRET

Visit of HRH The Princess Royal
to Kensington Girls' High School

THIS DAY – FINAL BRIEFING
Security arrangements and timetable unaltered

Final notes

Names of Local Authority guests:

Councillor David Best (Leader of Council), Neil Gyte
(Director of Education), Councillors Peter Rush,
Lilian Rowlinson-Jones OBE, Nigel Waters.

Security State as at 09.00: YELLOW

No especial problems are foreseen regarding HRH's
visit to Kensington Girls' High School.

However, new traffic arrangements have been made
for onward journey to Leicester Square (see separate
briefing).

This visit officially ends at HRH's exit by car from
Lippard Street into Kensington High Street. Duties
taken over by evening shift.
Ends.

KENSINGTON W8

By six-thirty on 15th October, Lippard Street looked as if it had been cleared for filming. Residents had been warned by the local police that their parking bays were suspended from twelve noon, and everyone had complied. The Kensington Traffic Division was notorious for taking no prisoners. But side streets were packed as tight as ferries with sleek cars, chained scooters and one white Ford Transit van. 'Road Closed' signs were at either end of the long street, and although the police standing by them were acting the friendly bobby, they had more on their belts than buckles; while at the school gates stood two police officers who looked burlier and meaner than the local force.

Kensington Girls' High attracted bright students from different backgrounds. Its catchment area included the homes of foreign diplomats and oil company moguls, so it was nothing to see a few CD and Arabic number plates on the school run. All nationalities came here, and where Augustin Baptiste and Laurina Modeste would have seemed out of place going into Cheltenham Grammar, they were an unremarkable part of the polite queue going into Kensington Girls' High.

A driveway ran from the street to the school building, where gracing the gates was the official board, newly repainted in gold on Oxford blue. Modeste had been there that morning, to make herself known again to Doug Way. She had arrived at his house on the premises as arranged at ten o'clock, but had kept her head down for the CCTV cameras. And he had been waiting, flashing his eyes, his teeth, his gelled hair.

'You been expecting me?'

'Oh, yes.'

'And is this where I'm comin' tonight – after everything's over?' She looked him up and down, lingering on down, in case there was any chance he had forgotten her promise of a good time to come.

'You ring my bell at the gate— '

'Man, I'll be ringin' your bell all right!'

'—And when I say so, give it a pull.'

Laurina Modeste just stared big-eyed at him. And so she was given her two tickets for that evening's visit by Princess Anne. She already knew the layout of the new drama block, the door to backstage and the quick way out. Posing as a prospective parent, she'd toured the school as soon as D had found out the location of their target – which is where she'd seen Gussie Beckford's name on a locker, with a sticker of the Jamaican flag on the door.

It's not the undetected crime, it's the unsuspected crime.

'I'll be seein' you later, then, Douglas.'

'Sure. Now get yourself off, lady. I've got to walk round the school looking normal.'

Laurina smiled at him. 'Mr Way, you won't walk normal for a week when I've done with you. You better lay in some supplies…'

And she'd gone, to come back now with her two tickets 'Guest of Mr D. Way.'

Now the audience was in, everyone seated as HRH The Princess Anne arrived. As one, they stood, while, casually amidst the formality, the royal visitor smiled and nodded her way along to her seat in the front. She and her party were in the centre while on either side of her – introductions, bows and curtseys – the other dignitaries sparkled their chains and badges of office.

Laurina Modeste and Augustin Baptiste had dream seats for their purpose, thanks unwittingly to Doug Way, who was hovering at the back of the audience in his best suit, trying to be matey with the royal detective. They were sitting at the end, two rows behind the princess and close to the door to backstage and the quick exit. She had passed them on the way in, and she would pass them the same way going out – well within touching distance.

They gave no clue that they were up to anything other than seeing the play. They stared at HRH as others stared, and they resumed their seats with the rest of the audience when the front row sat down: except that neither of them smiled, where most did. They sat and waited as the house lights dimmed and the lights came up on the open stage.

And Augustin Baptiste fidgeted just a little on the end of the row as he checked that he'd got the something special in his pocket that he was going to have to use.

CONFIDENTIAL FILE

Fran Scott – her story 3
(transcribed from tape)

I want to be clear about this – I've got nothing against the woman as a woman. With all the scandalous crap around the Royal Family, old Anne's one on her own: she does her own thing, goes her own way, speaks her own mind – and I admire her for that. But why make that sound like some virtue? Tons of people are the same – most of my teachers, for a start, definitely Mum. It's only because she's prepared to be herself amongst a lot of boring royals that makes Anne stand out at all.

No, I wasn't dancing with excitement at the thought of her seeing our show the way some of the others were. The big, exciting performance for me was going to be the last night; although I doubted if Dad would make it – but I really wanted Mum and Mike to see the play. Especially Mum. She's a historian, she's into women's stuff, she's written a couple of good novels about strong women, and this play we wrote about girls in Holloway Prison was strong stuff, and researched by us. Not inside, of course. They don't let you in there, not even on Work Experience – but we got to read the things the female prisoners wanted to write to us about: like, the smell of the place, the quarrels and fights, the loneliness inside their heads, and the love they found. It has to be terrible to be locked away from the world like that, out of control of your own life, where you can't even take paracetamol for a pain without going to see the Medical Officer. You've got to be a really nasty criminal to deserve Holloway – but some of the loving acts between them made you think twice.

So I really wanted Mum to see it.

They emptied the school around lunchtime with just us left inside. That's when the nerves kicked in, a couple of silly arguments and the giggles and raucous laughs about nothing much funny. Gussie had a sausage in her packed lunch and you'd have thought she could have gone on at the Comedy Club. Kenny Richards had to take it off her in the end, and eat it.

But we sobered up for the dress rehearsal, and that went OK. Mr Way the caretaker hung around a bit near the dressing room but Kenny shut the door on him – he's creepy, that man. Then it was a load of technical stuff for us in the drama block while some police mooched around the school and finally checked under the seats where Anne and her lot were going to sit. 'No gunpowder?' they asked. 'No need!' said Kenny. 'This show's going to bomb badly enough!' Ha ha.

And then in no time at all it was clear the stage, house open, beginners please, dim house lights on the royal white face, and 'up we go!' as Kenny says.

To 'come down' just under an hour later – me at the end of the line for the curtain call and running off into the office on my own – to land in this horrific situation...

VICTORIA SW1

Across London, Dennis Scott was in his Westminster flat. He called it his Westminster flat, but it was in Victoria, not far from the Catholic Cathedral.

Tonight was a busy 'red box' Tuesday, all his ministerial papers for reading and signing in the two hard red leather document box cases handed to him by his department as he left the building. He never slept at home on Tuesdays, which was the night before he always faced Home Office questions in the House of Commons – and especially not this one. There were rumours – rumours that happened to be true – that an announcement about Claude Chaumet would be made the next day, and both he and the Prime Minister might have to square up to a fight about it in Parliament. The big issue at the moment was still the sex scandal of the Prime Minister and his private secretary, but Magayana was warming up on the side, although neither of them wanted to say anything definite about what was going to happen to Chaumet until after the Home Office decision was made public at six p.m. By then police would be guarding Claude Chaumet under house arrest and would stay there until he was deported – on charges of abusing Britain's hospitality and breaking diplomatic rules.

So during this Tuesday afternoon, Home Office officials had briefed Scott on the line to take in Parliament, and the following morning Scott would brief the Prime Minister; everything was in his government red boxes beside him on the sofa.

Except, Scott didn't get this vital work done. As he sat with a scotch, skilfully catching peanuts he was throwing into his mouth, he suddenly stopped, and frowned. On the top of his pile were the personal letters he'd slid out of his postbox here. The first was a small, white unstamped envelope addressed to Kilty. Scott frowned. Very few people called him Kilty these days, only a couple of chums from Winchester and Cambridge, and they used his real home address when they wanted to be in touch.

He slid the end of his Parker pen under the flap and took out the paper inside.

'Good God!' As if it were white hot he let go of the paper, dropping it onto his knees without reading it. OK, no anthrax, but it was a death threat or some crazy request, using the old trick of cutting words from newspapers or magazines and sticking them onto cheap paper.

He swore again, picked up the paper, swapped pen for peanuts as he fed while he read. He could have screwed it up and flung it across the room into his litter bin – another of his games of skill – but he didn't. These days forensic might want to test it for fingerprints or DNA. He adjusted his glasses to focus on the message, mildly curious only because some clever Herbert had used a nickname that few people knew.

And he choked on his peanuts as he read what the message said.

FRANCES sCoTT D IEs
IF You D o NOt
TeLEpHoN E 078081720635
DEATH ALso IF POLICE oR
GOVERNMENT TOLD

'God!' again. Dennis Scott checked his watch as he leapt up, peanuts and paper everywhere. Ten thirty. He scooped up his mobile from the top of the television and pressed the direct dial for his Kensington house.

His wife answered immediately. 'Fran?'

'No, it's me. Where is Fran?'

'Not in yet. I thought this was Fran, Gussie's parents were going to bring her home. She's probably celebrating after the—'

'She's not in?'

'No, I'm waiting for her, getting a bit anx—'

'Stay there. Now listen. I'm coming home.' Dennis Scott was pushing into his shoes and shuffling for the door; just remembering to scoop papers into a red box. 'Don't phone anyone about Fran. Don't mention her. There's a problem—'

'*Dennis!* Is she all right?'

'I don't know. She's gone missing. Could be some hoax. You hold on there. I'll be home in ten minutes.' Dennis Scott cracked his phone shut, stuffed the threat into his pocket and rushed out of the flat.

And at the other end, Caitlin Jones's legs buckled under her and she found herself fighting to get out of the armchair into which she'd collapsed.

CONFIDENTIAL FILE

Fran Scott – her story 4
(transcribed from tape)

It smelt like the end of the world, like the stink of dying. I really thought I was being killed by this choking stuff. They were backstage when I slipped off the end of the curtain call line-up, they came from behind. Someone grabbed me and held this rag over my mouth and nose and all at once I'd got no legs. It hurt under my arms where they pulled me along, but I tried to fight them, I really tried to fight them. And, nothing! All of a sudden I had no strength and I went under, down into some foul blackness. All I can remember was coming round a bit and being lifted up into the back of a tinny van somewhere.

I don't know how long I was under. Only seconds, it seemed like, but anaesthetic's like that. But when I came round, this woman – I could smell her musk – she held this gassing rag over my face for longer and harder, and there was no way I could tell how far they drove me in the back of that van. Except, the first thing I heard over the sounds of the van was an aeroplane – a very loud aeroplane.

I started to kick and struggle – were they abducting me abroad? – and then I saw the big woman through the light from the windows, not very clear, she'd got some balaclava thing over her face – but I'd got no fight in me, I was too woozy. All I could do was try to scream but I couldn't, I hadn't got the breath, I hadn't got the voice – like in a nightmare.

She said, 'Leave it! Leave it! You'll hurt yourself!' Her eyes were staring out of that mask. I couldn't pick out anything else in the dark, but seeing that much scared me more, she had a real desperate look. We swayed about in the back as the van rocked along – and I heard that loud aeroplane again, or another one. Very loud. Landing. Was I going to be stuffed into a crate and freighted away?

I started to scream, now I did find the breath – and a bit of strength to kick and try to punch her in the face. But she came round at me again with that foul rag – and while I tried to bite her, have her filthy hand off, she pushed it onto me, and down I went, down, down into that dirty dropping darkness.

And I can still taste it in my mouth. I don't reckon it will ever rinse away...

(tape clicks)

HOUNSLOW, MIDDLESEX

It was still light but with a flat white sky like tracing paper hiding the aeroplanes coming in to Heathrow. The row of business premises was deserted, the only life the glimmer of light reflected in an oil patch on the concrete road. This was a nine-to-five industrial estate – a few wide gates, some thirties style buildings in cheap, sharp bricks – and like the rest, the building outside which the white Transit stopped was empty.

Augustine Baptiste slid open his door and jumped from the driver's seat. Without looking to left or right but with his head up and acting as if he belonged there, he walked across the cracked pavement and put a key into the lock at the foot of the garage shutters that fronted the street. There was no fiddling, the lock had been oiled. The shutters opened, and he drove the van in. Nothing was said. Laurina Modeste came from the back when the shutters were closed and together they carried the snoring girl down a short corridor from the garage space into a back room with a steel door.

The small room had no window, just a low wattage bulb for light. A mattress with a thin pillow and a couple of blankets lay on the floor along one wall. There was a tubular chair with a split canvas back, a new plastic bucket, and in a corner a small, dirty sink with a single tap; otherwise nothing. For ventilation, an air vent up near the ceiling brought in stale air from the corridor.

They laid the girl down, dressed in her 'Holloway inmate' jeans and top. Her mouth was open, there was lipstick on her teeth from the force of the chloroform rag, her stage made-up face showing blue shadowed eyelids, liner beneath, and a hint of blush through which her pale skin showed.

Laurina Modeste threw the blanket over her, left it as it landed. 'Light on or off?' she asked, but not like a caring mother to a child put to bed; it was a sharp question to Baptiste.

'On, or she'll think she's died.'

'So?'

'She's not the enemy, she's the ammunition.' Baptiste let his partner out of the room, leaving the light on, and locked the heavy door.

In the narrow passage outside, Laurina Modeste walked ahead into a kitchen. 'An' this is terrorist business, remember? Don' you get soft an' cosy on no schoolgirl.'

'Don't worry yourself!' he hissed into her back. 'If it comes to killing, it ain't gonna be you an' it ain't gonna be D – you just fix on who's got to do that, the same way I'm doing.'

An exchange unheard by Fran Scott as she opened her eyes in the room they'd just left; not unconscious at all, but acting it in a way to make Kenny Richards proud.

KENSINGTON DRIVE W8

Michael Scott came downstairs at the sound of his mother crying. His parents had rows like everyone's, but his mother wasn't a crier. He stopped outside the living room door at the sound of a sudden shout.

'*We've got to tell them!*' his mother cried.

'We mustn't! We can't!'

'We can! It's the history of blackmail. You *tell,* you always have to *tell!*'

'We *don't*! Not till we hear more.'

Michael went in, ran into his mother's arms, his Manchester United pyjamas crumpled and creased. 'Mum! What's the matter? You're crying!'

'It's Fran!' Michael's mother hugged him to her, crushed him in a great shaking grip. 'She's late.'

'She's late,' his father repeated. 'After the play. Celebrating somewhere, no doubt. Gone back to Princess Anne's place!' He was walking about the room like an exercise freak.

'Not really?'

'No, not really. Somewhere, we're not sure.'

Michael looked from one to the other, at the ministerial red box flung onto the sofa. 'Is that why you've come home?'

Dennis Scott nodded.

'Have you been round the school?'

'*No!*' The parents said it together.

'We should!' his mother said. 'Or phone Gussie's mother.'

'No we shouldn't – and, Michael, you mustn't say a word!' his father warned.

'Why? Will she get into trouble?'

Caitlin wailed again. 'Oh, Fran…'

'No, she won't get into trouble.' Dennis Scott stopped his pacing and turned his son to face him. 'And no one must know, you understand? She's been foolish, staying with a friend. Gussie. Changed their plans.'

'That'd be OK,' Michael said. 'Gussie's mum's nice.'

'And you're not to worry about her. And not to say anything to anybody about her...sleeping over.'

'Is it against the law, then?'

'No,' his father said, 'but it's not what a responsible member of the Home Secretary's family is expected to do, off the cuff, like that. So not a word to anybody, you really understand?'

'OK.'

Caitlin got up and went to the kitchen to check Michael's medicine, Mysoline, for his epilepsy. 'You've taken your tablet?'

'Course.'

'Then back off to bed. Dad and I have got some things to talk about.'

'About not knowing where she is? Is that why you're crying...?'

'Don't be silly!'

Michael frowned. '...because she can't be celebrating somewhere – *and* doing a sleep-over at Gussie's...'

'Please go to bed. There's nothing to worry about.'

Michael went to the door, a small slight figure who couldn't fill his Man U kit. He turned back, tight, tense face. 'She's gone off, hasn't she? She's run away, or something!'

'What?' from his father.

'Why would she do that?' from his mother. 'Has she ever said she would?' She stared hard at him.

'She's happy enough, isn't she?' Dennis Scott gruffed.

Michael faced his father. 'She said she wouldn't ever vote for you!'

'She doesn't have to. She's *got* me, I'm her father. But if she possesses a mind of her own, I'm pleased...'

'If she's got *anything*!' Caitlin cried. 'Dennis, *tell them!*'

'No! I know what I'm doing – which is not to panic.' At which Michael was steered firmly up to bed by his father. Returning, Dennis Scott opened his mobile phone and spoke into it, stilted, to a recording machine. He gave no name, just his mobile phone number.

And Dennis and Caitlin Scott sat, stood, paced, drank coffee; and waited.

> TEXT MESSAGE RECEIVED 22.00 HOURS
> TO D. SCOTT
> CLDE CHAUMET NOT AWARE THS ACTION
> WE ACT ALONE FR MAGYNA
> DNT DPORT THS MAN
> WE HAV UR DORTA
> WILL DIE IF DPRTION HPPNS
> DIE DIE DIE
> NOT THREAT BT PROMIS

Dennis Scott read it. His wife was upstairs with Michael, who couldn't sleep. He saved the message and waited for Caitlin to come downstairs again.

'He's off,' she said. But the look on her husband's face froze her where she was. The glowing mobile phone in his hand, held like some zapper, was all she could focus on.

'You've heard?' she asked.

Dennis Scott nodded.

And as Caitlin took it and read it, her scream split the house loud enough to wake Michael again, only the Mysoline he'd taken earlier preventing a severe epileptic fit.

CONFIDENTIAL FILE
REUTERS NEWS AGENCY
HOME OFFICE ANNOUNCEMENT:
09.00 16th October

EMBARGOED UNTIL 21.00 16th OCTOBER

Rt. Hon. Mary Mills, Under Secretary of State, Home Office, to announce the deportation of Claude Chaumet, leader of the People's Democratic Party of Magayana, with effect in fourteen days.

Government statement continues: HM Government has regrettably decided that it is to enforce its strict rules on foreign politicians' conditions of residency in the UK. Mr Chaumet has actively continued his campaign against the government of Magayana, a friend and ally to the UK, whose troops have fought alongside British forces in several conflicts, but he has limited entitlements in this regard.

International rules on residency require foreign nationals operating in an official political capacity to abide by a personal code of conduct that Mr Chaumet is considered to have breached. These breaches include abuse of car licensing, telephone, official postage and local rates and tax concessions.

Mr Chaumet has fourteen days in which to appeal to the Home Secretary. Should an appeal fail, the deportation order will be immediately effective.

For further details contact press officer, Home Office, 2 Marsham Street, London SW1P 4SA tel. 0870 000 1585, fax. 020 7273 2065
www.homeoffice.gov.uk e-mail public.enquiries@homeoffice.gsi.gov.uk

Statement ends.

SOUTH BANK SE1

Ben Maddox saw the Reuters print-out as it came in 'on the wire' on the Wednesday morning. Within fifteen seconds he was out of the newsroom and knocking on Kath Lewis's door. As she called him in she said, 'I know – I've seen it.' Her phone was in her hand. 'I'm buzzing you now.'

'So – they're going to do it. Deport Chaumet.'

'Or they're keeping President Gomez in the loop by *saying* they're deporting him.'

'Why? What's to be gained by doing that?'

'Search me.' Kath Lewis was staring hard at Ben, almost through him as if to some problem on the far side of the room. 'Could be some deep game they're playing.'

Ben shook his head. 'I've been out there, Kath, and I can tell you – they want him home to kill him, and because they're up to something with our government, we're going to let him go. See – as an official opposition leader he can still go to the United Nations on Human Rights grounds to get their sugar policy investigated.'

'Their game being...?'

Ben shrugged. 'Some international scam, you can bet.'

'Their website any good?'

'Magayana? Checked it, it's bland. Sort of place where a tribal massacre is "local unrest".'

'No private briefings from our government on what's going on?' Although Kath Lewis would have heard them from someone on the Westminster beat.

Ben shook his head. 'Whatever Britain's up to, it's deep, covert, secret...'

'Why use one word when three will do? But you're really up to speed with this, aren't you?'

'Shan't know, Kath – till someone overtakes me.'

The producer retreated to her desk, looking past Ben again to the far side of the room where on the wall there was a photograph of Len Wyatt holding a BAFTA mask, an award for television journalism.

'Call me stupid, but with our top faces busy on the Prime Minister scandal, I was wondering whether you were up to doing an interview with Dennis Scott...'

'I tried to get one. He threw his daughter at us.'

Kath eyed him as if she really wasn't too sure about this. 'I'll take some flak from upstairs, but I'm actually wondering, studio. A Zephon News face-to-face.'

At which Ben's stomach flipped. *What?* Studio interviews with government ministers were for the really big boys and girls.

'If you're up to it...?' Her question to answer, or his? 'We know you haven't built a following yet – no viewer knows or cares about you – so I could use Maggie Turton or William Finch, trusted, household names...'

'Sure, like lounge and drawing room – with me coming out of the loo...'

Kath was not amused. 'But Maggie's not political, and Bill's...' She left that sentence to hang private. 'You don't want to do it?'

'I do! I do! But will *he*? Won't he expect a bigger name for a studio interview, a man in Scott's position?'

Kath cut in quickly, she'd clearly thought this through. 'No, he'll jump at it, because he'll expect an easy ride. So are you up to giving him otherwise?'

'Course I am! And as it happens, I've got an interview request to the Home Office that I drafted last night – but not for me. I thought Bill Finch, thought you'd go for a bigger boy.

It's ready to go when you've approved it.' He slid it out of an inside pocket and gave it to her.

Kath Lewis looked at her hands. 'What made you do it last night?'

'Because Chamet's deportation had to be announced some time. The way Scott reacted on the doorstep, things were clearly building. I thought we ought to be ready for it.'

Kath Lewis picked up a sheet of paper from the desk. 'So did I.' She handed Ben her draft request, printed off her laptop. 'We'll use mine. I know the language of these things better than you.' Without reading it, she dropped his into her waste bin.

Ben read hers. 'That's OK,' he said. 'Mine's better argued...'

Another Kath Lewis smile, weakish. 'Exactly. They'll know where you're coming from before he gets in his car to the studio. My way he won't.'

Ben nodded gracefully and handed back the paper. Kath Lewis put it on her desk in her slapping space, but gently. 'You've still got a hell of a lot to learn, Ben Maddox.'

'Thanks.' Ben said it so that she knew he was thanking her about everything, the assignment, this chance.

But there was no more response from Kath Lewis: she was buzzing through for her secretary, moving on.

BY HAND

Mrs V Wellington MA
Headteacher
Kensington Girls' High School
Lippard Street
London W8 5EW   Wed. 16th October

Dear Mrs Wellington

Please accept my sincere apologies for not informing you sooner that my daughter Frances has been taken ill with a respiratory problem, as a result of which my husband and I have sent her to an aunt in the country for the time being. We hope that the country air will enable her to make a speedier recovery than in the polluted air of London.

I trust that this information will enable Frances's absence to be an authorised one.

We are especially conscious of Frances's absence from the current drama production, but we take comfort from the assurance of Gussie Beckford that there are understudies for the remaining performances tonight and tomorrow. Sadly, neither my husband nor I will be able to attend as we had planned.

Yours sincerely

Caitlin Jones

Caitlin Jones
mother of Frances Scott

CONFIDENTIAL FILE

Fran Scott – her story 5
(transcribed from tape)

Where was I? Oh, yes, they thought I was still knocked out. So I played dead till they'd gone – I reckon it gives you a chance, anyway. People not killed in massacres play dead, but I never thought I'd be in this hole myself. Anyhow, I stayed deep asleep, as if I was still unconscious from their stinking chemical. Also, when I opened my eyes I came over woozy again and wanted to be sick so it was better all round to lie still.

God, I was scared – still am, but it's deep down in the gut now like some deadly disease you've got to live with – till it gets you! I'd read about all this sort of hostage thing, we were all warned about it by Special Branch when Dad got his government job – but they tell it like the airline people going through their safety stuff, serious faces and 'just in case' voices, where landing on water is never a screaming vertical dive. But now that dive's happening, really happening! I've been dragged off, knocked out, locked up, but not tied up – not even handcuffed to a radiator – so I'm thinking I must be in some really strong hideout somewhere.

And some terrible thoughts – are these people suicide terrorists, are they going to blow me up with them; are they fanatics like those Iraqi killers; is that man going to rape me; or am I going to be left here to rot – die without air or food and water? Then I think, how can I get out of this place? Then, what are my parents doing about this? Then – and really urgent now – where can I go to the toilet?

I open my eyes so-o-o slowly, just in case it's all bluff and one of them's still standing there. Already, through my eyelids,

I know there's a light on. I look around, draw my legs up to kneel on the mattress, gradually get to my feet. And just for a moment I'm going to faint, I come over all dizzy again, it must have been the chemical they'd knocked me out with.

But I don't. I take deep breaths and coming off the mattress onto the concrete floor, I tread quietly round the room, which is like one of those mechanics' places at the back of a garage. There's no window but it's got a titchy sink. And no lavatory but a bucket, which is new – and behind it a roll of lavatory paper. That's one question answered, so I take advantage of the answer, a quick wee, and rinse my hands under the cold tap.

I'm scared, I'm really scared. Are they political? Extremists? Are they idiots – do they think I'm Princess Anne? Are they going to kill me? Are we all going to go up in some big explosion – is the van I came in packed with explosives? I'm thinking all of this while I take the place in, which is what you do first according to the Holloway women. You see where you are then you start thinking how long you're going to be there; but at least those girls know, at least they know the sentence...

(A long pause)

The door fits flush and looks like metal because it's got rusty bolts in it, and the lock takes a monster key, going by the key hole. I bend down to look through it, but all I get is an eyeful of dark, it's got to be covered on the other side. On another wall up above a radiator there's an air vent, but it's dusty, cobwebby, no fluttery movement – so either it doesn't go to the outside or it's blocked in somehow.

And up higher still, heard not seen – can't see them of course – are these aeroplanes. Continuous. So now I reckon I've got to be near Heathrow. I haven't got my watch, I took it off for the play, but counting in what I think are seconds, those planes are coming over every minute or so. No other airport's that busy, is it?

Suddenly, terror! – there's a key in the door. I dive back to my mattress – as in they come. Him and her. And the sight of them gets me screaming, really screaming! I scream louder than I've ever screamed before, they look like killer terrorists. Suicides. He's got a black baseball cap pulled down over his face and a cowboy neckerchief over his mouth and nose. She's in a white cotton balaclava, like Ku Klux Klan without the witches' point. But thank God they aren't in monkey masks – I'd have died there and then – and no guns, no knives.

'Shut up that row!' the woman says. 'You're not bein' heard.'

She's got a lilt to her voice, but not London West Indian, something different. And, big and strong, twice me, she grabs me from off the mattress, gets round behind and holds me facing the man. Tight. Professional.

What the hell are they going to do? I try to kick him, but he's too close, I can't get the movement. His bandit face is right in mine, all I can see is the shine in his eyes.

'Calm yourself down, now. You're where you can't be heard an' can't be found.' Something like that, he says, the same lilt she's got.

His eyes are close, I want to spit at them, but I don't dare, not unless he comes at me with his hands.

'Any luck, you're goin' to be away from here an' back home 'fore you use that bucket again...'

So can they see into this room? Which could be a trick because you feel exposed and vulnerable then, like a prisoner with a peephole in the door.

'...given your father sees sense!' the woman comes in strong.

I hold my head back, keep my mouth shut tight. So it's political. Or is it money? No, it can't be money.

'But you got to convince him you're here, alive. So—'

The door behind him is open – can I make a run for it? But in seconds he's backed off me while the woman still holds on tight, he's gone out and come back in again with something, locking the door behind him.

It's a tape recorder, the cassette sort.

'This here's to help us, an' help you,' he starts on. 'You make sure, inside your father's head, that you're alive an' then he'll do what we want. Else, it's us has to do somethin' terrible we don't want.'

God! He's said the worst! What I thought. And suddenly I feel numb all over; I can't feel this woman holding me any more, and all around my mouth it's like a dentist's injection, and I'm cold, shivering cold.

'You get yourself together, an' you say into this, "I am" – an' you say your name – "an' I'm alive, Thursday night ten o'clock." You get that wrong – or you shout something else, we wipe it, and we wipe you across the mouth, and you do it again. You got that?'

I can't nod, but I blink.

'Right.' He fiddles with the thing, doesn't know it all that well and she starts clucking behind me, but then he gets it running. He holds it up level with my face. 'Right. Shoot.'

I take in a breath, shaky, like in the middle of crying, almost hiccups. 'Hello, Mum and Dad,' I start out saying.

'Shit, no!' He prods the thing off. 'I'm telling you what to say. "I am—" Don't you hear good?'

'No, that's OK,' the woman comes in, over my shoulder. 'Let her say that.'

The man stares at her, stares back at me, doesn't say

anything. Just switches the recorder on again, and nods.

'Hello, Mum and Dad. And Mikey.' He looks at the woman again, but she must be giving the thumbs up. 'It's me, Fran Scott, and I'm alive on Thursday night at ten o'clock.' And I screw shut my eyes and just hold my silence till I hear the recorder switch off and then their names hit me – Mum and Dad and Mikey, my family – and I lose my legs from under me, and I wail, cry, shake, and fall down onto the mattress, curled up tight into a ball, seeing my mother's face.

And that's when it hits you. This isn't drama in the drama block, this is real, this is happening to me!

And I'm scared! So scared!

(tape clicks)

ZEPHON TELEVISION

South Bank Studios – London SE1

FAX   FAX   FAX   FAX

TO MEDIA COMMUNICATIONS UNIT, HOME
OFFICE 020 7273 2065

This is to confirm the Zephon Television request for a
live interview with the Secretary of State for Home Affairs,
the Rt. Hon. Dennis Scott MP, on a News Special
programme at 21.00 hours on Thursday 17th October at
Vauxhall Studios.

The main subject under discussion to be the Minister's
concerns in light of the deportation decision by the
Immigration Service regarding Claude Chaumet, the leader
of the official opposition in Magayana, pending appeal to
the Minister.

The interviewer will be Benjamin Maddox, a Zephon
Television staff reporter.

Kathleen Lewis

Executive producer, 'World View' and news/current affairs.

The interview was on! It was going to be the biggest thing Ben had done so far – a one-to-one with the Home Secretary: subject, an explosive issue of the day.

On the Wednesday evening before the House rose, a brief announcement about Claude Chaumet's pending deportation had been made to Parliament by Dennis Scott's deputy, Mary Mills. But neither Kath Lewis nor Ben Maddox wanted her on the programme. Scott was the man in Zephon's spotlight. And this would be exclusive, one of those 'breaking stories' that would only hit everyone when it broke. Ben knew that everyone else was running round with the scandal about the Prime Minister possibly getting a divorce and leaving his children. Who lived in Downing Street then? OK, interesting to some but not important in the order of world events. So Zephon would make the mystery of Britain and its links with Magayana the next really big thing. Len Wyatt had been quietly on to it, and now so was Ben Maddox, in the big time!

Kath Lewis rehearsed Ben in the studio, let Bloom Ramsaran watch as training for the future. Ben would introduce the deportation subject to camera – first draft script written by Ben and polished by Kath – then Ben's interviews filmed in Magayana would be run, the 'package' as it was called, and the fifteen minute slot in the news programme would finish with Ben's live interview with the Home Secretary.

They ran through without cameras, Kath down on the studio floor, then again with the cameras, Kath up in the control suite, with the director calling the camera shots and the mixing cues.

OK. Ben's earpiece gave him Kath's timing, and with the studio manager supplying Scott's answers he brought the interview to an end right on the second. Very professional.

'Great timing!' Kath said.

'Thanks.'

'Otherwise, crap.'

'What?'

It all went quiet while Kath Lewis locked-in the camera positions with the mixers and floor manager and made her way from the control suite down onto the set.

'You looked either scared shitless or ready to punch him on the nose. And what for God's sake happened to your voice?'

Ben pulled out his earpiece. 'Too soft, too loud, too cockney?'

'Too high. Your register, love. It was all up in your nasal cavities – sounded like a voice-over for a Bugs Bunny cartoon.'

'Cheers.' Ben shuffled his papers. And he heard Bloom Ramsaran say 'Aaah…' somewhere out of the lights.

'Relax, breathe, be yourself. You're not giving him a job interview, or the sack. You're at Euston in the first class lounge politely asking Virgin Customer Services what time the next Manchester train is, and why the last one was cancelled, and, oh yes, what are they going to do to stop it happening every rotten Friday. Now show a flash of teeth. And do it with the confidence in your voice that you know the railway timetable and the scheduled repairs *and* the staff rotas ten times better than they do.'

'Is that all?'

'So, let's go again…'

'Again?'

'Again. Then get round to his house and doorstep him early evening; get your name in – so when he meets you eye-to-eye in the studio he knows you, calls you Ben. That way you're a known factor, it gives you an air of authority, credibility for the viewer...'

And suddenly Ben wasn't nervous any more. A rollicking in front of Bloom Ramsaran and the crew followed by a slice of good advice left him where Kath Lewis wanted him.

Up for it.

KENSINGTON DRIVE W8

From the Home Office diary it looked as if Dennis Scott would be getting back to his house in Kensington Drive around five o'clock. The programme would go out three hours later. So Ben didn't bother to hide down the area steps today; he wanted to be seen. He was alone, no Jonny Aaranovitch, no camera, just a small digital recorder – Zephon did radio news as well as television. His only problem was, what the hell was he going to ask the man? What question could he put that he wouldn't put later? Kath Lewis had left Ben to work that one out.

He decided to go for another tack altogether; Home Secretaries had more than one thing on their plates at a time. There was law and order, prisons, the justice system, the royal family, tons of stuff. So Ben hit on prison reform, the scandal of young people in prison cells who felt so helpless that they hanged themselves; an Asian boy had died that week in prison custody in Leeds; yes, he'd ask the Home Secretary about that.

Good evening, Minister, I'm Ben Maddox, we're meeting later at Zephon Television – but I wonder if you have a comment for our news bulletin about... That sort of thing: it was all for show, anyhow.

But Ben didn't get to ask the question because Dennis Scott didn't come home. Or he hadn't left. There was a policeman on the doorstep as usual but he wouldn't say a word about any comings and goings, he never would, of course. And by a quarter to six Ben was starting to get anxious about his own time. He rang the studio on his mobile, did they have any news of Scott's whereabouts? Was he going to the studio straight from the Commons or from his Department? Had anyone seen him? *Would he turn up?* But no one had any information, everyone at the other end was very laid back about it.

If Kath Lewis was concerned, she didn't show it. 'He'll turn up. He knows we'll make a meal of it if he doesn't – and I've got Bill Finch's piece on prime ministers and mistresses up my sleeve...'

Ben wound up his wires and put his recorder away, started to make for the entrance to the Drive and Kensington Gardens – when a young black girl came hurrying past him towards the Scott house. She went straight up the steps to the policeman – who must have known her because he stood aside to let her ring the bell.

Walking on across the road, Ben stayed behind a tree to see who would answer the door – but like Downing Street, you hardly ever see, it's opened by the Invisible Man. The girl went in. Ben waited, but not for long, because in no time flat, the girl came out again. She looked at the policeman and shrugged – before walking off up the drive, fast.

A friend of one of the kids? A maid? A government messenger? Ben reckoned the girl could be anything – but he wanted to know, especially as she suddenly stopped at a plane tree, put her arm round it, and with a puzzled look on her face did a full circle as if she was making up her mind about something. Either to return to the house, or go? And Ben could see that she was deciding to go; but before she could, he was there, with her.

'Hi!' he said. 'Ben Maddox, Zephon Television.' He flashed

his press card; and, as it mostly did, it bought him a second instead of a slap in the face.

'That's a funny old business,' he said, tossing his head behind him towards the Scotts' house. 'Not there!'

It was a chance. A flyer. And it worked.

'Only gone to her auntie's,' she said. 'Not well.' She shrugged, the way she had at the policeman, but she was frowning.

'This is Frances? You look surprised? You didn't know she wasn't there?'

The girl eyed him suspiciously. 'She's just a schoolmate to us,' she said.

In other words, end of interview, this was private life and the girl was schooled not to talk about her high-level friend.

'Still, a surprise. You were meeting her?'

'*Acting* with her, actually. Supposed to.' The girl looked at her watch, turned. Now she was going to run.

'Tonight?'

'School, it's in the papers, I'm not telling you anything you can't find out.' And now she did go. She waved an arm like a celebrity caught in the street and went, running fast.

Ben watched her go, then went to find a cab. A girl of Frances Scott's age just not showing up for a school performance? Was it nerves – or was she really ill? At which a sudden spurt of his own nerve juices hit him, because he'd got his own big show to do. But as he went, and amid the rehearsing of his Dennis Scott questions in his head, one name kept recurring.

Jonny Aaranovitch.

He'd said that something about the girl wasn't right, hadn't he? Now she was missing an important school performance. Food for thought – but only a starter because Dennis Scott was the main course and Ben had got his own first night to get through.

DAILY POST, FRIDAY 18 OCTOBER

LAST NIGHT'S TV
WORLD VIEW✴✳✳✳✳

Is 'World View' worth its place on the plasma screens of the pubs and clubs where our leaders gather?

Last night's offering was a going nowhere tetchy interview between Home Secretary Dennis Scott and new-boy 'dish of the day' Ben Maddox. A likeable enough young cub against an old political bear who without cracking a smile said the clever equivalent of 'no comment'.

The subject was Magayana. Where? MagaYAWNa, more like. It's something TV's Len Wyatt – the late, great – had his teeth into but should have been laid to rest with him. The leader of Magayana's opposition party is one Claude Chaumet, whom the immigration people want to kick out of the country.

'Why?' asks our cub. 'Because he can't behave himself.' The bear puts it simply. The elderly foreign national has walked roughshod over all the diplomatic rules, abused his stay, and the government's had enough. Then, three cheers for a good decision for once, say I. But not our Ben.

'Aren't you just trying to keep the President of Magayana sweet?' the cub whines. 'Why shouldn't we?' comes the answer. 'President Gomez is an ally.' Then the cub makes some clumsy 'sweet' references back to his own filmed interview – shown earlier – featuring an unhappy sugar farmer from the north, whose crop isn't being exported this year.

The bear gives him a lesson in world trade. Doesn't young Maddox know that there's a global sugar glut? Hasn't he heard of food mountains rotting in warehouses when world trade dictates that it should? This is no different, and no more sinister.

Grow up, young Ben – or we'll grow out of TV programmes like 'World View' and its spawn. You may be pretty and clean-shaven, but this format's got whiskers on!

© jillyprime@dailypost.co.uk

At least Ben didn't have to go on and do it again tonight, with a matinee thrown in on Saturday afternoon. Theatre actors who get bad reviews have to go on doing it till the end of the run – but with television it's over and done with. Small consolation, though, for the kind and condescending smiles given to him by Zephon people from the doorman up to Kath Lewis. Although hers wasn't so kind, wasn't so much of a smile, more a grimace, as she put down the paper – the same look she'd had at the disappointed debriefing the night before.

'We didn't have enough to hit him with!' she'd said. 'And we should have foreseen how he'd respond to the Magayana package. We needed Claude Chaumet speaking for himself.'

'He's under house arrest.'

'So we get a camera in down the chimney. We dig and find! We're not a mouthpiece for government statements from straight-faced suits!'

Which Scott had been, hard and pale as a marble bust and 'somewhere else' in his head – but still seeing off the interviewer.

None of which was personal about Ben – who thought he'd handled the live interview quite well, as a professional – it was just Scott's blocking of every line of questioning, not personal until this morning when Ben heard Kath telling her secretary, 'We can set people up to be the next Len Wyatt, but it comes down to foresight and being in the right place at the right time. Homework – and luck. Maddox has got to do one and make the other. Or what about Bloom?'

Well, God, hadn't Ben tried to be in the right place at the right time? Hadn't he interviewed President Gomez's spokesman in Magellan? Hadn't he doorstepped Dennis Scott twice – and was it his fault that the guy didn't show the second time? And could Kath consider that perhaps Len Wyatt hadn't really got a story, that the sugar situation in Magayana *was* the way Scott said it was, that Claude Chaumet might be the villain of the piece? And was he meant to have overheard what she said about Bloom – to a secretary? Was she setting up the two new kids to be tigers at one another's throats?

He threw a few notes around on his desk, he looked at the TV monitor showing *Zephon 24/7 News*, he started on the daily papers – avoiding his bad review – to see what fresh item he might suggest at the mid morning story conference. And the way a word will sometimes fly out at a reader like a thrush from a thicket, the name of Scott's daughter's school suddenly leapt from the newsprint of a small diary item down in a bottom corner of the previous day's *Evening Standard*.

ROYAL HOLDS UP PREMIERE

Princess Anne held up the start of the new James Bond film last night when she arrived late from a previous engagement. Her excuse? A school play at Kensington Girls' High School. 'It over-ran,' she said, 'but was far too good to walk out on.' Good for you, Ma'am. At least one royal sometimes goes to serious theatre and stays to the end.

Ben stared at the item. Two nights ago. Frances Scott would have been there, that was the play – and it was performed for Princess Anne. And last night she missed the second performance, unwell. Was there anything significant in what this girl was about? Was she anything to do with the strained and tetchy look Scott had carried with him into the studio and through the interview? Aside from Magayana, was he having daughter problems? Was she into drugs, drink, a lairy boyfriend? These things happen, even to royalty and government ministers.

And how unwell had she looked on Jonny Aaranovitch's camera? Ben hadn't picked up on anything like that, but had that been what Jonny had spotted, the something that was puzzling him? Or was there something imperious about her that said she'd do the show for royalty but wouldn't bother with an ordinary audience?

Ben found the tape and slotted it into the machine; he ran it over and over again – Dennis Scott coming out of the house, waiting impatiently on a late daughter, the girl hurrying to the car with her sports bag.

'Not that again!' Bloom Ramsaran had come up behind him. 'What is it with you and that girl? There's a word for people like you.'

'And one for people like you.' Bloom wasn't his best vision of loveliness right now, however tall and striking she was. 'Haven't you got a film to go to?'

Bloom leant on Ben's shoulder. 'This one's good enough if it's got you hooked.' And she changed from cheerful cocky at Ben's bad time the night before to pro-journalist. 'What is it you're looking for, Maddox?'

Ben's eyes didn't leave the running tape. Should he tell her or not? Might she take his story over, was Kath half-serious? But he found himself telling her; there was something about Bloom that opened him up.

'Jonny reckons there's something odd about her. Girl going to school. Something doesn't fit.' He heard Bloom's breathing close in his ear while she watched the tape run though again, just forty-eight seconds of it.

'Well, that's obvious, isn't it?' she said.

'Is it?'

'The nails. Look at those fingers. She's wearing acrylic black nails, or black nail varnish. Laddettes at my school wore it, but I bet it's not sanctioned at Posh Girls' High.'

Ben squinted to check it himself. Bloom was right. The girl's fingers were witch black. 'Well, she's in the school play,' he said. 'If she's playing a punky woman...'

'Or a toddler round my way... Yeah, she wouldn't have time to go to the nail shop, or do her nails in make-up, they wouldn't dry in time. She'd have to have had them done at home.'

Ben switched off the video. 'Is that all?' he said. 'Some mystery! And she looked fit and well to me. Did she look to you like someone about to be so unwell she's got to be sent to an aunt's to recover?'

'Nope. But then Ben Maddox doesn't look like someone who'd let her Home Secretary father walk all over him, does he?'

On which note, Bloom went, blowing a kiss. And Ben went out onto the river front balcony to swear – and just for a moment to contemplate throwing himself off it into the Thames.

KENSINGTON DRIVE W8

As far as the world was concerned, they all went down with a twenty-four hour bug – Dennis Scott, Caitlin Jones and Michael. The Home Secretary cancelled departmental meetings and a dinner with the head of the prison service, the author told her publisher she was taking to her bed and wasn't to be rung, not even if a TV adaptation was confirmed, and Michael was kept off from school. In the house in Kensington Drive the Scotts kept themselves close, like after a death, but letting Michael continue thinking that his sister had run off, pressure of exams, they said. Desperately, they waited for the next move from the person who had sent the text message. Dennis Scott kept his mobile charged, on the hour, every hour; the BT phone line was kept free; and the e-mail checked regularly for messages. People who helped in the house were phoned and told not to come in, in case they caught the bug, and the minister was too ill on the Thursday night even to take a phone call from the Prime Minister. It was like that.

But not like that. Because although they waited and waited and shared their anxiety, Scott and his wife argued fiercely all the time about what they were going to do about the kidnap.

'You've *got* to tell someone!' Caitlin kept saying, she wouldn't let it rest. 'You can't keep this to yourself – *ourselves* – when you've got MI5, Special Branch, the rest of Scotland Yard and all the police forces up and down the country who could be looking for her!'

'You saw the bloody text message! If we speak, she suffers...

'God! You saw what happened in Iraq! They'll do it anyway, won't they?' Caitlin's face was distorted with the helpless anguish of a victim's mother. 'We'll find her body in some alleyway!'

But Dennis Scott was firm. 'No, they're not like that. There's been no public demand, no video tape for the TV stations. This is them, and us. Me!'

'So do what they want, then! Give in! Let this bloody Chaumet stay! Go against your lord and master randy prime minister and allow Chaumet's appeal. Now! Not in a fortnight's time – in a minute!'

And worse. Words flew like crockery, and Dennis Scott was accused of being every craven coward under the sun, putting his job before his family, showing what a self-centred, arrogant bastard he was: upstairs and downstairs, in their separate bedrooms, through the hallway, in the kitchen, below in the cellar and out in the conservatory, everywhere around the house he was a shit of the first order.

'Next move!' he kept saying. 'We wait for the next move!'

'Which could be to the undertaker! It's *your* next move! Let Chaumet stay! You say you've got assurances he'll come to no harm back home...'

'I say because *they* say! I do have some integrity!'

'Huh!'

And Michael heard the lot, what he was meant to hear and what he wasn't; and the look on his face when Fran's exam worries were mentioned one more time was of undisguised disdain.

'Just get her back!' he wailed at his parents. And, clutching at the hope that fiction holds, 'Get old Poirot in, or those private people...'

At which, in the kitchen making yet another cup of coffee, his mother rounded on his father again. 'That's it!' she said. 'Michael's said it – go to Krol!'

'Over my dead body!' Scott flung back.

'Over *her* dead body if you don't!'

'No!' cried Michael.

There was a long, silent pause with Caitlin staring at Scott and Scott applying himself to the crucial business of milk and sugar.

'Anyhow, who is this Krol?' Michael wanted to know.

'Big American firm, private, does detective stuff for big business...' his father told him.

'Well, then!'

'Well, then nothing! We're not going there, not yet, not me! Not the Home Secretary!'

An obvious cue for words to fly again flew, chipping and breaking over Dennis Scott; divorce threatened, and the breaking of ranks. Bugger him, Caitlin Jones would go to the police herself! Until he was forced to make her a promise. Krol it would be, but in his judgment, when the time was right. He was the Home Secretary, any decision on deportation was his and his alone, finally – and the kidnappers knew that. If he went public on this, the government would have to refuse to give in to their demands, states always did. He was the kidnappers' best hope on this, and, right now, playing for time was his family's best hope, too.

Another hot coffee was made; in which state of unhappy truce Scott announced that he'd have to go back into the world the next day or everyone would wonder what was going on. And the three of them went each to their own private places, where none of them would see the others cry.

ZEPHON TELEVISION

Transcript of telephone conversation,

Ben Maddox to Kensington Girls' High School 020 77276 4114

FRIDAY 18 OCTOBER

Unidentified voice, presumably a school secretary:
Kensington Girls' High School. Good morning.

<u>Ben Maddox:</u>
Good morning. I'm Ben Maddox from Zephon
Television. Is it possible to have a word with Vivienne
Wellington, please?

<u>Secretary:</u>
The headteacher's in a meeting at the moment. She's
very busy all morning. Did you say Zephon Television?

<u>Ben Maddox:</u>
Yes. We're doing a follow-up on the opening of your
new drama block by Princess Anne – we picked it up
from the *Evening Standard*. We thought it might make a
news item for our London programme.

<u>Secretary:</u>
Ah.

<u>Ben Maddox:</u>
Only, when I used to go to school we were always after
sponsors to fund the new lighting dimmers or curtains
or audience seating. The Marks and Spencers Green

Room in the Princess Anne Theatre – that sort of thing...
(laughs)

Secretary:
Perhaps you'd better have a word with Mr Richards, he's the head of drama.

Ben Maddox:
Mr Richards?

Secretary:
That's right. Kenneth Richards. (*Pause, sound of computer tapping*) He's not teaching at the moment. I'll put you through.

Ben Maddox:
Thank you.
(*Sounds of telephone transfer*)

Kenneth Richards:
Drama department, Ken Richards...

Ben Maddox:
(*After identification of caller and company*) ...We might like to run a piece about your grand opening, local news only, of course, but Princess Anne making James Bond wait because she was so held by your play – that's a story, isn't it?

Kenneth Richards:
Off the record – they were told the running time and her office got it wrong. But, yes, she did stay to the end, and of course we're thrilled about it.

Ben Maddox:
Any comments she made?

Kenneth Richards:
(After a pause) No quoting royalty, you know that.
Gracious. She was very gracious. There.

Ben Maddox:
And the show was on again on Wednesday?

Kenneth Richards:
And last night. I'm frazzled, thanks!

Ben Maddox:
(Laughs) I bet. And how did you cope for two nights
without one of your stars?

Kenneth Richards:
OK, thank you.

Ben Maddox:
That was Frances Scott, wasn't it? I hear she was taken
unwell?

Kenneth Richards:
(Another pause) That's confidential. You must know who
she is...?

Ben Maddox:
Sure, but...

Kenneth Richards:
She's not your story, is she? If so...

Ben Maddox:

No. Oh, no. It's just that if we film a scene for our spot and she's well enough to be in it, we have to clear things with the Home Office.

Kenneth Richards:

She's not in school, but the set's still up.

Ben Maddox:

Must be really ill. Did she get through to the end – on the night?

Kenneth Richards:

Yes, and that's common knowledge.

Ben Maddox:

And went home after the royal line-up?

Kenneth Richards:

About then. And that's not me saying, don't you quote me, the people outside knew. No one has to leave before the royal guest, but I think they made this exception.

Ben Maddox:

Her parents took her home?

Kenneth Richards:

No, they were coming last night. Again, that's not me saying – the 'Kensie' ran that item. Anyway, you'd better be snappy if you want to come in today, it's a question of calling the girls out of class...

Sure. Well, thanks Mr Richards. We'll be in touch
soon if we can come. But we wouldn't want to add to
your frazzle.

(The line goes dead).

HOUNSLOW, MIDDLESEX

Laurina Modeste looked up from her mobile phone.

'Anything?' Baptiste wanted to know. He was at a small
stove, brewing vegetable soup in an old enamel saucepan,
hunched over his heating.

'D wants the tape, to get it to the man...'

'Where's this?'

'Terminal One. Half an hour.'

Baptiste swore as the soup ran volcanic up the enamel of
the saucepan. He came to the table and poured it into an
earthenware bowl.

'That for her?'

'She's got to eat.'

'So've I.'

'Well, you're goin' out – you can bring us in Kentucky.
There's a place down the front, 'bout a half mile.'

'You want your suit pressed or your shoes shined while I'm
at it, boss?'

'No, Kentucky'll do...'

Laurina got up, looked to the ceiling. 'Dear Jesus, I don'
know who's the worse off, her or me. Solitary's got to be
better than bein' holed up with you. No talk about things
outside of what we're doing, no *nothin'* outside of what we're
doing!'

'An' you fully realise what we're doing? This has gone

past the stealin' of a van! Person can't think about other stuff with a girl lyin' prisoner in there!'

Laurina just gave him a look as she checked herself in a small specky mirror above the sink. Anyway, today she was neither made up nor in the frame of mind she'd needed for getting into the fantasies of Doug Way, but meeting D meant she had to tidy herself slick and respectable. 'Unlock the door an' I'll take that to the girl, you can't carry and lock at the same time. Then see me out to the street, OK?' She picked up the bowl of soup while Baptiste fished the big key to the cell from his trouser pocket. And without another word, but as security conscious as Guantanamo Bay, the food was taken in to their prisoner, their faces covered.

SOUTH BANK SE1

When Ben put the phone down after speaking to the girls' school he picked it straight up again and got on to Meera, who was an editor at Allman Books.

'Meer, what do you know about Caitlin Jones's last book, *Nelly Mabel Powell*?'

'Not a lot, only what you had on her website. Good reviews, if I remember – about a poor girl, suffragette, torn between family and belief. The old story…'

'Have you got a mate in the office who edits that sort of historical fiction – someone who might know someone who's got Caitlin Jones's private number?'

'Ben, I warned you about this…'

'It's her, not the children, I swear.'

There was a pause. Ben could see Meera's beautiful face, staring at the wall, making a decision. Then, 'Hold on.'

He tapped his pen on his teeth, not sure now where to go on this story. Speaking to Caitlin Jones was just a possible; so was getting a camera down Claude Chaumet's chimney – figuratively speaking, so was getting back to Jesus Guimet the sugar farmer in Magayana for more information from that end. Otherwise, the whole thing really could be spiked and forgotten – except Kath Lewis hadn't taken Ben off it, nor given him another assignment today.

'How're you doing?' It was Bloom Ramsaran, over his shoulder again, trying to take a look at his notes.

But he had put a hand on them; he'd already smelt her Thin Ice perfume. 'Doing OK, how about you?' He moved the phone to his other ear, so Meera wouldn't be next to Bloom when she came back. He didn't like people this close to him, not where their flicked-up hair tickled his face – or so he would claim.

'I'm waiting for a real job!'

To which Ben didn't have to reply because Meera came back. 'Caitlin Jones has got her own dedicated phone in the house so that book people don't have ministerial hassle. You mustn't say where you got it, but do you want the number?'

'Three guesses.'

Meera gave it to him, and Ben thanked her and finished the call – too cramped at that moment to end with any word of love. Now Bloom stood off. And now, of course, something seemed to fit…

'You got a few minutes?' he asked her.

'Got a few.' She looked across to a tidy, not to say empty, desk. 'Waiting for the American Golden Globe details to come in – then it's all hell let loose.'

'Reckon you'll go over there?'

Bloom shrugged. 'Who pays for the rude dress? We'll buy a package off Sky. So, can I do something for you?'

And Ben told her. She could ring Caitlin Jones, woman to woman, ask her about her new book, say she was researching for a possible news item linking *Nelly Mabel Powell* with voting on the internet at the next election – from suffragettes to surfers, that sort of thing. Which could lead to a throw-away question about whether Caitlin and her husband ever argued about these things indoors. Still woman to woman. And was she as happy as he was about the pending deportation of Claude Chaumet? How would Emily Pankhurst have viewed a possible violation of human rights?

Bloom stood, nodded, made a couple of notes – before facing him, as tall as he was. 'You're using me because I'm a woman.'

'That's right. I said that. Isn't this how we're supposed to work, using the best person for a particular job?'

'And when you do get some success with this story, will Bloom Ramsaran feature somewhere alongside the name of Ben Maddox?'

Ben laughed. 'Speak to "Captions".'

Bloom stood looking at him for a full five seconds before she told him. 'OK, I'll do your call.' And she turned and went to her phone, every move of the way followed idly by Ben as he went back to wondering whether he'd got a firework of a story, or a dud.

METROPOLITAN POLICE

KENSINGTON POLICE STATION

<u>DESK DAY-BOOK</u> – Friday 18th October   (extract)

His Excellency Mohamed Sabbar, Moroccan Ambassador to Britain, private resident at 33 Newchurch Road, off Lippard Street W8, complained at an inability to park his official CD vehicle in his reserved resident on-street parking space, fronting property, on Tuesday 15th October.

Background: Due to closure of Lippard Street to parked and through traffic on 15th October – reference visit of HRH The Princess Anne to Kensington Girls' High School, Lippard Street – residents' vehicles were obliged to park in streets off, including Newchurch Street.

Ambassador Sabbar complained that a Transit van, white, reg. X01FKM was blocking his parking space on his return from the Moroccan Embassy at 19.00 hours. He had to pay for public parking beneath Kensington Town Hall. The said vehicle was removed some time before 23.00 hours when his housekeeper checked again.

Ambassador Sabbar complained that police and traffic warden presence was insufficient to protect the interests of local residents. He has also complained to the headteacher and governors of Kensington Girls' High School for not providing neighbourhood parking on the school premises (ie, playgrounds).

Complaint logged: 11.15 hours by WPC W318 Ashcroft, L.

CONFIDENTIAL FILE

Fran Scott – her story 6
(transcribed from tape)

They bring me this soup. Yuk! But isn't yuk good enough sometimes? Well, I've got hunger pains, except this rolling over and over could be scare and fight and loneliness – and sadness, self pity, and bloody anger! It all happens down there in the same place.

The woman brings it in, he guards the door, both in the same disguises as before. I think she'd just as soon throw it over me, but she puts it on the floor. No bread. No spoon. Just this soup.

He turns away for a second – and I do it! My anger wins, and the injustice, and I make the break! I scoop up the bowl and throw it at him hard as I go for the door. I've been planning it all night, I'm not going to be anyone's pathetic prisoner! It was going to be the wee in the bucket but hot soup will do.

I go for the door as he's swearing and clawing at his scalding neckerchief, but then she's got me before I can reach it. She grabs me and swings me round and slaps my face hard and throws me down on the mattress. Then she gives me a big kick in the back.

'Stupid bitch!' she shouts, blowing out her balaclava with the words. 'Don't you even put it in your stupid head!' And she's on me, all her weight like some female wrestler, she's pinning me down like Gussie in the show only not for show. She's hurting me. 'You're here, and you're staying!'

'Let me go!' I shout back at her. 'I've done you no harm!' And then I start to cry – God, I only have to start to cry…

'You think that's the only door? You think you've got one chance in hell of getting out of here?' And she laughs; and she takes hold of my cheek and pinches it, pinches it, pinches it hard. 'You got a brother.'

Not a question. So I don't answer. But what she's just said, and hurting me like that, that suddenly stops me crying.

'It's you we got. But when we don't have you, we'll have him!' And she gets up and walks out, the man standing there all soupy, but she just shouts at him, 'Lock this door!' And they go.

And I curl up on my mattress and think about what she said, about my brother. And it hits me, hits me hard. She was telling me to behave, for the sake of Michael. My Mikey. So I know I'll do it. I'll have to do it. If it's me taking it, or him, it's going to be me.

But when I'm out of this I'm going to find these two – this prowling man and this bully of a woman – and I'm going to kill them. Yes. Yes! I'm going to bloody kill them both...

(tape clicks)

HEATHROW AIRPORT, TERMINAL ONE

The viewing platform on the roof of Terminal One is a chilly spot to meet in October, a natural 'hoods up' place. Binoculared men with sandwich packs and long range cameras make ticks in small notebooks as planes land on one runway and take off from the other. Down below, aircraft nose in and push back from the gates, petrol tankers rumble and catering vehicles scamper.

The breeze ruffled the fur of Laurina Modeste's hood as she climbed the final steps to the platform. Her man was there already, binoculars up, watching the arrival of a Virgin jumbo, landing with a puff of black tyre. He was tall, in an old-fashioned camel-coloured duffle coat, hood up also. As the 747 taxied on down the runway he swung the binoculars back to the sky to focus on the next inbound flight, headlights on, a smaller Airbus.

Laurina Modeste came up beside him. 'I brought your sandwiches,' she told him. 'The best. Club.'

He didn't waver from his following of the Airbus. His face was so masked by the hood and the binoculars he could have been Old Father Time, or Death.

'What filling's in it?' His voice sounded neutral, with the sort of 'somewhere else' accent a poor actor might use to play anything from an Irishman to a South American.

'What you wanted. With God's help, everythin' done like you asked for.' Laurina gave him a Tupperware box about fifteen by twenty centimetres and club sandwich deep.

'No trouble getting it?'

'No trouble.'

'Uh-huh.' The man slipped the Tupperware box into the bag at his feet and went back to his aircraft spotting.

Laurina waited a half minute then turned away to go back down the stairs to ground level, no further instructions received but her report given, and delivery done of the tape they'd made of the girl's voice.

Only when she'd gone, did the man the kidnappers knew as D, crouch to his bag again and transfer the tape into a small cassette recorder. He fitted miniature headphones into his ears and listened to the recording. Then, switching to record as a jumbo came in, all but drowning his voice and completely masking any accent, he uttered two words. 'Ten' and 'days'. But his tone was urgent, threatening. And he quickly packed up and went.

There were certain things for masterminds to know that footsoldiers needn't.

HOME OFFICE, MARSHAM STREET SW1

Dennis Scott's ministerial office was oak panelled but the walls could have been ears, the way he reacted when his mobile phone rang. Two secretaries sat at the big polished desk, one with Scott's diary poised, the other with a pile of files she was talking him through, the top one marked 'Claude Chaumet'. This Friday morning they were discussing next week's agenda, but the mobile phone tone was now, now! Scott answered it with streak speed, waving his staff away and out of the room, leaving their things.

'Scott.'

There was no 'Hello' or 'Hi', no direct voice at all at the other end, just the click and hiss of a tape starting to run. He drew in his breath and waited for what he was about to hear.

'*Hello, Mum and Dad.*' Scott screwed his eyes shut tight; he knew this trembly, frightened voice so well. '*And Mikey.*' He looked round the room, checking the shut door, lowered his head towards the desk, the phone pressed tight to his ear.

'It's me, Fran Scott, and I'm alive on Thursday night at ten o'clock.' And then a sudden click, followed by the sound of a roaring storm or an earthquake or a huge aircraft close up – and, just audible, two words in a voice that sounded as if it came from the other side of the grave. 'Ten days!' And a swift cut off, like a light extinguished.

'No...!' he groaned as he fumbled to 'missed calls' to get the caller's number. But no number had registered.

Immediately, he went to his office door. 'Not to be disturbed!' he called round it.

'Yes, Minister.'

Now he tapped in Caitlin's phone number at home. It hardly rang once before it was picked up.

'Yes?'

'Dennis.'

'Yes?'

'Get Michael away.'

'What?'

'Get Michael away. To Lydia's. Scot... You know where.' He'd half said the destination before he realised that the line might be bugged.

'Why?'

'I'm coming home. Fran's OK—'

'Oh, thank God!'

'She's not, you know... free. But I've heard her voice. I'm coming home.'

'Dennis!' Caitlin shouted into the phone. 'You've got to tell someone!'

'I'm coming home, all right?' And he switched off, to rush for the door and tell his people his wife was unwell again, relapse, call his car, he was taking an hour out.

CONFIDENTIAL FILE

ZEPHON TELEVISION

Transcript of telephone conversation, Bloom Ramsaran to Caitlin Jones

020 77591 2814

FRIDAY 18 OCTOBER

Caitlin Jones:

Yes?

Bloom Ramsaran:

Hi! Could I speak with Caitlin Jones please?

Caitlin Jones:

Who's this?

Bloom Ramsaran:

My name's Bloom Ramsaran, Zephon Television Arts Programme, and I wanted to ask you about your marvellous new book *Nelly Mabel Powell*...

Caitlin Jones:

No thank you, not right now.

(The line goes dead)

BEN
NO GO JONES
NO SPEAK UPTITE
C/OFF
BLOOM

BLACKHEATH SE3

Ben got the message as he walked up through Greenwich Park from the Docklands Light Railway, heading for Westcombe Park Drive. Something peculiar was going on, he knew, because what author wouldn't want to talk to television about their latest book? Even Caitlin Jones? Meera spent her life trying to get her publicity people to fix media interviews for writers.

Anyway, he was on another tack right now, about to be Father Christmas – going down a chimney. He'd rung his brother Patrick at the Yard – caught him in a St Katherine's Dock pub waiting to meet a contact – and asked him what police presence there might be for someone under house arrest.

'Depends who it is,' he was told. 'Remember General Pinochet of Argentina, sent home on violation of human rights charges? He was living in a private estate, walls and gates, a top people's compound, made life hell for the celebs who lived there...'

'This one's a minor foreign politician on car parking offences.'

'Ah, your Chaumet bloke. Down in Blackheath?'

'You said the name, not me.'

'Oh, he'll warrant a bobby on his doorstep, all a bit token. More likely a bobette.'

'No hairy armed guard?'

'Have you seen some of our WPCs? But definitely no flak jackets required.'

'What if he wanted away from the rear? Escape over the garden wall?'

'That would definitely lose him his appeal case.'

'Cheers, mate.'

'I could be wrong!'

Already, Ben had checked on the visitor situation, the likelihood of him just going in to Claude Chaumet to do an interview – but a visit would have required special permission from the Home Office and, strangely, that department wasn't answering. So Ben's plan was simple. In the office he had blown up a street map of the area, one of those detailed local government maps that show house numbers and garden boundaries – and he had worked out which side to come at Claude Chaumet from.

The back.

A walk past on the opposite side of Westcombe Park Drive proved that brother Patrick hadn't been wrong. There was a bobby on the porticoed doorstep of number thirty-three, looking bored out of his mind – duty shifts like that had to be worse than a museum attendant's, Ben reckoned. He saw the map in his head. These were detached houses built a road away from Blackheath itself, with generous walled gardens, and Chaumet's house was only two along from the junction with an intersecting road. Ben took himself to the corner and round it. As he'd expected, there was a six foot wall in London brick that faced onto the pavement, and, as he'd hoped, there was no barbed wire or broken glass on top of it. And also as he'd hoped, there seemed to be no one about in this residential road on an October Friday morning.

He couldn't do anything about the chino trousers and Guccis he'd gone to work in, but in the Zephon office he'd swapped his reefer jacket for a jeans bomber: casual gardeners wore that sort of thing, didn't they? Now he took a good look at the wall, sized it up. After university he'd done a mad couple of months with Zippo's Circus, where he'd laboured, clowned, and learned a few circus skills – and he knew the way to get up onto the wall was to come at it along the pavement, not across it face on. He'd take a good run, leap with his left leg kicking up like a high jumper, throw his hands onto the top of the wall for grip, and swinging his right leg above his head – his knee onto the top brick – he'd pull himself up.

With a last covert look around, an activity covered by pretending to poke at the state of the brickwork like a builder inspecting it, he suddenly ran for the wall as if he were going for a rope in the big top – put everything into it, total effort. A leap, a swing, a grab, and Ben was up there, lying flat along the wall looking down into a neat, lawned garden. Quickly, he dropped into the shrubs beneath him, and using them for cover he checked for sounds or sights of a nosy Neighbourhood Watch. But, nothing. This house seemed empty right now, no one in, but for the benefit of anyone spotting him from anywhere else he walked across the lawn slowly as if he were checking for worm casts, as if he had permission to be there. Builder turned gardener.

From then on it was over a scratchy fence to the next empty garden, Guccis nearly dunked into a water feature, and across that one. Now he stopped as a strong grab of doubt suddenly got hold of him. Next door would be Claude Chaumet's. What if brother Pat were wrong – what if there was a police presence at the back door, or even Chaumet's own security people? Cautiously, he stood on a stone bench and looked over the fence – to see a smallish, elderly black man raking leaves off the grass. Alone, and raking fast and impatiently the way non-gardeners do.

'Hi!' said Ben. 'They're early this year. The leaves, falling.'

'Not rain enough.'

The man didn't seem suspicious, just angry with the leaves, somehow; the gardener pose worked – until Ben used the bench to make an easy climb over into Chaumet's garden.

'Excuse me! What are you doing? This is not your garden!' Chaumet's eyes looked at Ben's hands for a weapon. Clearly, assassination, murder or state execution could come in any form. He poked his rake at Ben, tines towards his face. 'Get back! Off! Go away!'

Ben jerked his head out of line of the rake and grabbed it. 'Hang on! I'm Zephon Television. Ben Maddox.' He flashed his press card at the man, who stared at Ben and slowly let go his end of the rake. Now Claude Chaumet seemed to recognise him. As he'd hoped, the man had seen the duff TV duel with Dennis Scott the night before.

'You have been in my country...' And he had seen Ben's Magayana film shot by Jonny Aaranovitch.

'Sure. I talked to your people. I saw the hungry kids

and the rotting canes. I want to talk to you, Mr Chaumet, I want to help...'

Ben could see Chaumet making his quick decision, saw him look back at his house and across at the fence, then at the sky in case there was a helicopter up there. And he must have decided the risk was worth it.

'Come, inside!' he said, and led the way through a small conservatory into a plainly furnished sitting room.

Assiduously, Ben wiped his feet along the way. When doorstepping was more garden hopping, good reporters didn't leave muddy footprints behind.

CONFIDENTIAL FILE

Fran Scott – her story 7
(transcribed from tape)

*He comes back on his own, not long after. I don't know
where the woman is but he acts differently, coming in, sort
of secretly, round the door – creepy, and I'm dead scared.
Well, I'd scalded him with soup so there was that to sort.
And if she isn't there, or she's letting him in on his own,
what's in his mind – some nice punishment for the girl?*

*I run to the bucket and pick it up, it's all there is in the
room that's anything like a weapon. But he just stares at
me with those needle eyes as he locks the door behind him.
He's cleaned up, different shirt, and this time a different
neckerchief round his face.*

'Put that down, I got enough washing, girl.'

*His hands are down at his sides, and he shows me the
flat of his palms. But the room's so small, he could be at me
with a quick grab.*

*Why trust him? Why should I? Eh? 'How do I know
what you're up to? You've got no right to keep me here!'
Get indignant – keep talking to them, don't wind them up
too much but don't encourage them. Never smile. Keep
yourself covered, and small – never stick your chest out.
Funny how you remember these personal safety lessons
when you can't remember pi-R-squared.*

*He leans against the wall by the door. He could be tall
but he's a bit stooped. Suddenly he puts his hand in his
back pocket and pulls something out. I jump back and
thump into the sink – but all he's got is a cereal bar, still
wrapped.*

'You done for the soup, girl. You want this?' He doesn't throw it, I've got both hands on the bucket so I can't catch it, but he goes over and lays it on the blanket, gently, like some votive offering. 'I'll go fetch you some coca to send it down.'

I say nothing. Best not to. He goes back to leaning. I get the feeling he's making up his mind about something – perhaps the worst, how to get at me without being dowsed in wee. Or what to say.

'Looks bad, uh?' he says as the bucket gets heavy in my hands. 'What we're doin'.'

'Looks bad? It is bad! Sodding bad!' I can't help myself – even though I mustn't rile him.

'I tell you this so you know,' he looks round at the door as if he shouldn't be talking to me, put his hand under the neckerchief to make speaking easier, 'this, what we're proceeding with, is for survival – a whole people's survival...'

'And what about my survival?' I'm too scared to throw this bucket at him, but God I'd like to! 'I don't count, eh?'

He just shrugs.

And now, I don't know why, I put the bucket down. Well, I do know, it's because of what he said. He's making excuses for what they're doing. And it is heavy.

And I suddenly hear myself saying things. 'What sort of person do you think I am?' Something like that. 'Powerful? Mighty? Important?' I stare at him, get his eyes across the room and keep them. 'If you're under the heel do you think I'd be on the side of your people's survival – or against it? Have you checked me out – or am I just the unlucky one?'

'You've been checked out,' he says. 'No luck come into it.' And he leans off the wall, starts fishing for the key.

'Well,' I say, 'if you're so worried about people, can I go to the loo? I can empty this pee down the sink, but not...'

He thinks about it. 'Later,' he says. 'You have to hold on, but if you can't...' and he looks at the bucket, shrugs again, '...that's for any emergency.'

And he goes. Which does tell me he's on his own. If there's a loo and they're going to let me use it, it can only be that the woman's got to be there as well. The Holloway people said the girls in Category A had to have two prison officers for escorting them around the prison.

And I must well be Category A. Or if I'm important enough to end up dead, Grade A Star...

And, Gussie, we'd laugh at that if I was back with you...

(sudden sobbing – tape clicks)

KENSINGTON DRIVE W8

'What is it? What have you heard?' Caitlin Jones faced her husband as he came pushing in through the door. Dennis Scott's public expression turned the burden of a ministerial post into a look not far from horror as he faced his wife.

'A tape recording, her voice!'

'Where from?'

'Don't know.'

'Was she crying? How did she sound? Tell me!' They stared into each other's faces ready to fight like angry cats if either said an unbalanced word.

'She sounded OK, not too bad, like Fran coping.'

'Scared?'

Dennis Scott took a deep breath. 'Yes, scared,' he said. 'But...alive...at ten o'clock last night.'

'Oh! Oh!' And as Caitlin made a deep sound like a mortally wounded animal they suddenly rushed at one another to hug as hard as people can, and to cry into each other's hair.

'Tell! We must tell!' Caitlin came out of it first. 'Forget Krol – go to Special Branch, they're clever, they know how to deal with this sort of thing. It's their job...'

But Dennis Scott was shaking his head. 'Not yet,' he said. 'Not yet. I think I can solve this my way, but I need a little time...'

The time he'd been given, though, the outside time, the ten days he kept to himself.

'Your bloody way! *Your bloody way!* This is our daughter...!' Now Caitlin *was* going for him, not the flying words now but hitting at him with her fists. 'You've got to get help! I tell you, if you don't, I will!'

'You won't!' He held firm, face into face, frightened her

with his stare as if she didn't know this man. 'That's…the…last…thing…you…must…do! For Fran's sake! She won't stand a chance if the SAS go storming in.' He grabbed her wrists, but not before he took a blow to the cheek. 'We get Michael away, and then you leave it to me. *I know!*'

'*You know!* You're useless!' She wriggled and squirmed to hit him again, but from the intense urgency of what he'd said some of the spirit had gone out of her, and the appearance of Michael, pale and shocked, rucksack over his shoulder at the top of the stairs, stopped a real fight from developing.

'What's up?' He came running down the stairs. 'Is Fran dead?'

'No!'

'No! Of course not!'

And they both hugged him, reassured him, the child who was safe and with them.

For now.

BLACKHEATH SE3

Whoever else was in Chaumet's house was keeping out of the way. Ben could hear the sound of someone upstairs, and he knew Chaumet had a wife, but no one came in to disturb them. Packing, perhaps. The room was neat and anonymous like a hotel sitting room, no one's real home; and Ben guessed that Chaumet hadn't been raking leaves for the sake of the garden – more for relieving his stress.

He was offered tea or coffee, which he declined – interview rule, the making of hot drinks takes people away, interrupts the flow, gives them time to reflect, make quick phone calls; journalists rarely say yes to a kitchen visit unless it's going to break the ice, or they're writing a 'profile' piece about someone's life style.

Chaumet sat him on a sofa and faced him across a marble fireplace from an armchair. For raking the garden he was wearing a crew-neck sweater, his elderly bald head coming up out of it like a tortoise. And he was slow and deliberate, too, no time for flash or wasted movement.

'I saw your programme, Mr Maddox. Your filming was by my home village.'

'Petit Fleuve?'

The old man nodded. 'And Jesus Guimet I know very well. My grandfather worked with his grandfather.'

'On the sugar?'

'The barges, both of them.'

Ben shook his head, smiled at Chaumet. 'I couldn't get much out of Dennis Scott. He's been shut up like a clam by someone—'

'That would be your prime minister.'

'And no way was he going to speak frankly. So, what's their game, in your view?'

Claude Chaumet stared across at Ben. 'First I must ask, what is *your* game? Are you a responsible journalist or do you need your story for the six o'clock news, anything will do? Are you honest with me?'

Ben met his gaze equally. 'Have you heard of Len Wyatt?' he asked.

'I have, but I could not meet him, it was the wrong time for me. And now things are different, this government has made its decision about me.' He waved a hand in the direction of central London.

'Well,' said Ben, 'you may have read it or not from what he said on air, but Len Wyatt was sympathetic to your cause, he was taking it up.'

Chaumet nodded. 'Yes, I read it in his manner. And I think I read it from you, but you know I have to be sure…'

'I'm trying to fill his shoes, on this story.'

'Another man's shoes are never comfortable till you mould them to yourself!' The elderly politician suddenly got up and went to a plain sideboard from which he took a folder. As he came back with it he looked Ben straight in the eye, a look of determination: Ben could see what a fiery young fighter this man must once have been. 'My mail is put in a deep hole somewhere, and if I speak on the telephone about anything serious the line goes dead. My e-mail is also dead, the provider has shut down my address.'

Ben knew the impotence that Chaumet had to be feeling; his parents had once done that to him when he'd been a stroppy teenager.

'But I have my cellular phone. They have not silenced that, yet.'

'And this got through?' Ben pointed to the folder in Chaumet's hand.

'I received it just before the house arrest, at the Paddington hotel, before a retired friend in the sugar business allowed me to come here to be detained.' From the folder he took a piece of paper. 'Mr Maddox, what do you know about Magayana?' Chaumet's voice was suddenly high and sing-song.

'About as much as you've seen in the programme. After Len Wyatt died it's been my project at Zephon, but I've only been out to your country once.' Ben realised that he sounded like a kid in primary school, back from a field trip.

'Well, Magayana has an interesting past.' Claude Chaumet tucked the folder under his arm for the present. Ben straightened his back to pay attention. 'Portuguese settlers were the first, a long time back in the fifteenth century. The native Americans already living there became slaves to them – apart from a little inter-marriage, not approved; no, not approved; but when sugar became the king the Portuguese needed slaves to work the plantations, more than all the native Americans put together, so they brought slaves across the sea from French west Africa. And these are my people.' Chaumet nodded, went on nodding as if he were marking the terrible times his ancestors had had. 'Then comes the revolution. At much the same time as the American civil war uprising, our plantation slaves claimed for their own the lands we had been working for centuries. In truth, we had seeded enough blood into them, had we not, for them to be ours? And we were strong and determined, and to save the revolution from spreading south where the white Portuguese lived, the government agreed to the transfer of the lands. Since then my people of the north – the Afro-Magayanese – have been the legitimate owners of the soil on which their fathers toiled.'

'That seems fair,' Ben said, 'but it's not the history of the world, is it?'

'Magayana still is a country divided,' Chaumet went on, as if Ben hadn't spoken, his eyes focused somewhere else, perhaps back in Petit Fleuve. 'Them and us, us and them. We have given the country wealth through our sugar, they the white rulers sharing the profits of our work through the government tariffs and taxes we pay, but we have still been the workers. Now, however, they are losing us markets deliberately, making useless our plantations so that sugar buyers will go elsewhere, driving us off by poverty, forcing us to leave our lands, sending us to lead tourist-pleasing lives in the slum quarters of the cities of the south, like the native American Indians...'

Ben stared at the man who had become animated, striking the folder, anger in his voice as he raked at the situation.

If only Zephron had been able to get him into that studio with Dennis Scott!

'Is that where the Amerindians fit in?' Ben asked.

Chaumet cracked a hand in the air. 'Except for just a small population in the west of the country who live their own original life; and a few inter-married on both sides. Not at all significant.'

'So your two main political parties are...?'

'Are racial groupings. White European, black African. And now we are about to be humiliated finally, because if we cannot sell our sugar the president can turn the wheel back on the revolution.'

'But sugar's what your country's about – till now. Isn't it? For the president, for everyone. If *you've* got no sugar income, *he's* got no sugar income.' Ben stood up, because his next question needed him on his feet in Len Wyatt's shoes. 'So what *is* under your lands that Jorge Gomez wants to get his hands on?' Surely this top politician had to have some idea?

Claude Chaumet shrugged. 'Gold? Diamonds? I can make only the usual guesses. They are both found in our rocks, but hardly sufficient to make a ding on a tin plate. I truly do not know...'

Ben folded his arms. He had been all the way out to Magayana to draw this same blank. 'So who was doing the drilling? Someone had to have been drilling...'

Chaumet put a hand over his eyes, shook his head. 'We do not know. There were guards, and plain-clothed trucks, if you understand me.'

Ben smiled, then frowned. 'But Gomez will definitely profit from *something* under there?'

'Oh, yes, definitely. If he cannot be stopped.' And now Chaumet was suddenly poking into his own chest. 'Providing that your government sends this meddling old man home to be dealt with, so he does not upset the neat and tidy order of things.'

'Upset it through the United Nations?'

'And the Court of Human Rights.' Claude Chaumet returned to the sofa but didn't sit. 'Now read this, please,' he said, finally opening the folder.

Ben sat and was given a sheet of paper. There was something handwritten on a cheap lined notepad. He read it.

My son, what can I leave for you?
My daughter, where is your dowry?
Your land is stolen beneath our feet
To a worthless crust of sucked sugar.

Son of my blood, daughter of my skin
Do not go down on your knees.
Take ruthless action against the foe
To keep your birthright grounds.

The land's first dwellers are dead and fled,
Bled into others' ways.
You will be next, dispossessed
By hunger and genocide.

Let some men take their political route,
Seek the world to engage,
But you wield the blade, cut it deep
Into the enemy's heart.

Force the hand across the sea
To let reason and justice prevail.
Strike at their sons as they strike at you,
Death they understand.

Ben looked up. 'Who wrote this?'

'A poet. A patriot. A fighter.' Claude Chaumet remained standing over Ben, his hand out to be given back the poem. 'So, what is he saying, Mr Maddox?'

Ben had no doubt. 'Someone like you can carry on the straight political fight, go on doing what you're trying to do through the United Nations...'

'And?'

'...While others – I presume, not involving you – must take direct action to keep you doing your job...'

'This is what I think. So how will they do this?'

Ben got up again, gave the paper back as Chaumet put out his hand for it, it was not for public release. He looked the old politician direct in the eyes, thinking back on the last two days when some things had seemed to be falling into place. He chose his words with care. 'I think they might already have done it.'

There was no response from Chaumet. Ben thanked him, made a note of his mobile number, and looked to the conservatory door to leave.

But Chaumet took his arm. 'But for me, for my work, Mr Maddox, you bring some hope. You are free. I am not, at present, and there is no one in Magayana who is free to do my work, they are all locked up. Keep digging, like the exploiters of my land. Because down there lies the truth...' And instead of to the back he escorted Ben to the front door. 'They changed policemen an hour ago,' he said. 'This one will think the other let you in. You are my solicitor, perhaps.'

'Dressed like this?'

'We are not very formal in Magayana,' Chaumet twinkled. Which had to be a rare sight, Ben thought.

Perhaps, somehow, he *had* brought the old man hope, as he'd said.

But was that what a professional journalist – even with attitude – was supposed to do?

GOVERNMENT CAR POOL – DRIVER'S LOG

ROVER 65   CAR CODE: HO/12

Friday 18 October

07.40 speedo 11,312 Garage to Kensington Drive W8 with Prot officer and return to Home Office, Marsham Street with Minister and Prot officer, no school deviation, arrive 08.25, heavy traffic Kensington area, speedo 11,318. Stand down, rest hours due.

11.13 speedo 11,318 Home Office, Marsham Street – emergency call – to Kensington Drive W8 with Minister and Prot officer, wait: Minister, Prot officer, Mrs Scott and son to King's Cross main-line railway station, wait: Minister and Prot officer to Home Office, Marsham Street, arrive

13.15, speedo 11,334 Stand down.

Friday no parliamentary business for Minister.

18.25 speedo 11,334 Home Office , Marsham Street to Kensington Drive W8 with Minister and Prot officer and return with Prot officer to Garage 19.05, speedo 11,341. Stand down.

Rest hour payment claimed for Minister's emergency call 11.13 – 13.15.
No incident report.

Signed: P.R. Bellamy, snr. Driver

Countersigned: L. Terrett supervisor

KENSINGTON CCTV CENTRE

Ben decided that there's a sort of mafia in the Met. police service of the pleasant, clubby sort. Police people know people, they've worked with them on division somewhere, or in a squad at the Yard, or on assignment, or maybe they go way back and trained together at Hendon. And whether in the uniformed branch or in CID or Special Branch, they'll do a mate a good turn if they can. Which, Ben knew, was so different from what happened in his line of work, where a matey hand usually had a grenade in it. Now he was being taken into the darkened CCTV monitoring room where much of West London was under Big Brother's eyes, and where ex-Detective Inspector 'Chubbs' O'Hara worked. Now out of the Met. he was at the London Borough of Kensington and Chelsea's CCTV Centre, but he'd been Ben's brother's boss years before on a long running illegal immigrant racket in the East End, where they'd got very close; so it was natural that he'd do his young 'oppo' a favour; and shortly after Ben had introduced himself to the council receptionist at the desk, the tall, thin 'Chubbs' came down himself to take him up to the monitoring suite.

After a few catching-up pleasantries, 'So you're the younger brother, eh?' and, 'How's our man?' sort of stuff, Chubbs said, 'Patsie tells me you're after looking at the Princess Anne tapes? Lippard Street, fifteenth October?'

Ben smiled to himself; it was always weird when other people had names for your relatives that you didn't use in the family.

'Yes. Fifteenth of October, between, say, six-thirty and ten pm.'

'Fair enough.' Chubbs led Ben into a darkened room which seemed very familiar to him, not a lot different from a gallery at the Zephon TV studios. There were anything up to twenty colour monitors in banks before him showing West London traffic scenes, as well as static cameras monitoring the pavement outside Harrods and a couple of porticoed doorways that had to be embassies. The operators were all busy, the only difference from those in a TV gallery being that producers and mixers sit very still, except for their hands and fingers, while these men and women were twisting on their swivel chairs between screens. But each of them had the time to turn and acknowledge Chubbs and Ben coming in, the general atmosphere relaxed but vigilant – again, very much like a newsroom.

'Anything particular you're looking for?' Chubbs asked him.

'Yup, Princess Anne's visiting a school, and a schoolgirl's behaving a bit oddly, not being seen where she ought to be seen.' Ben didn't know what Patrick had told Chubbs, but you never let out more than you have to, not even to friendlies. Neither did he want Chubbs to think he was wasting his time. And this was all just doing what reporters do when they don't have a line to follow – they go over all sorts of material, however unpromising.

Fran Scott had appeared in the play for Princess Anne. The next day her best friend had been surprised that she was dropping out of the rest of the performances, supposed to be unwell – so unwell that she'd been sent away to her aunt's! So had something happened after the show that night? Was some jealous understudy bullying her not to perform? Or was there a gang of girls who wanted to teach her a lesson? Or perhaps some boyfriend who wanted to run off with her – or some young teacher? Those things did happen. A look at the CCTV might eliminate something, although it was all probably a waste of time.

Already knowing from brother Patrick the tape that Ben wanted, Chubbs was feeding it to play in a free monitor, running it through the fourteenth of October like a mayfly's life flashing past.

'You can run it back and forth like this, slow it down like this, zoom in and out like this, and freeze it like this.' Chubbs showed Ben the right buttons to push as he ushered him to sit down. 'So I'll leave you to it. Cup of tea?'

'Cheers. Coffee, please, no milk, one sugar.'

Chubbs went, after a fairly searching look round all the screens – and Ben was left alone to watch the CCTV of the night that Princess Anne had gone to the Home Secretary's daughter's school. The time display ran forward at the top left of the screen in minutes, seconds, and tenths of seconds; while the images running fast forward or back were in black and white, settling into a high resolution colour when the tape was slowed to real-time speed.

Ben hardly blinked as he sat there just like the other operators in the room, a temporary member of the club. On the screen at 18.50 he saw a queue of parents and friends on the Lippard Street pavement, waiting to go into the school, tickets in hands. He zoomed in on faces, but there was no one hanging about – no young male, no gang of girls – as if they were waiting for the show to end. Running forward, at 19.20 he saw sleek government cars arriving and the arrival of the Education and Arts ministers, shortly after the local mayoral car with the Kensington crest had come, and at 19.30 to the second, the royal limousine without a number plate came into picture carrying Princess Anne. He saw the flashes of a press camera; and already knew the local newspaper report that had gone with that photo; with nothing in it to give any clue of an incident, nor any local 'colour'; just a bland and typical bread-and-butter piece about the new drama block. He ran through an hour or more of Lippard Street empty of vehicles, a rare sight in London, and a couple of bored police officers trying to keep alert – metres and metres of nothing happening.

And then suddenly he saw what he hadn't expected to see. Yes! It was something he hadn't hoped for, what he wasn't happy to see – but so much what he wanted. He had a lead! The time on the screen was 21.25 and 3-something seconds. The sequence he saw stood alone: there was nothing, then this, then three and a half minutes of nothing again until HRH came out.

He ran the scene, froze it, rewound and ran it again. And what he saw was quite clear – three people emerging from the school entrance and going away from the camera along the pavement up Lippard Street, backs to the camera. But two of them were taller than the third, and were walking on either side of her. They were in long dark coats, one an H&M duffel going by the furry hood, and the other with a black leather cap pulled well down. Female and male? And why was Ben thinking of the middle one as 'her'? Because she had an arm dangling round the shoulder of the woman in the duffel and was being helped along the pavement as if she were ill, her feet almost dragging – and, quite clearly in the excellent CCTV image, the fingernails of the visible hand round the woman's shoulder were black! An image he'd seen before. An image that Jonny Aaranovitch had seen and that Bloom Ramsaran had identified as being the unusual element about Frances Scott going to school that morning.

'Seen anything yet?' Chubb had brought Ben his coffee. He looked at the screen that Ben had run on to audience coming out. 'Anything jump out an' catch you?'

'No, nothing helpful, I'm afraid.' Ben took up his coffee, sipped it. 'Sadly.' He shrugged. 'It was just a chance.'

'Chances bring charges, sometimes, that's what I always used to say. But Patsie wasn't very hopeful, to be honest...'

'No – but if you get anything else, anything local to the school that's unusual, any of the residents come up with anything, could you give Patsie a bell?'

'Will do. I'll ask some mates in traffic police, and I'll have a quiet word with Kensington nick. Anything on our plot we share.' The old boys' club at work again.

'Cheers.' And Ben felt bad, being allowed to be a member of the club, and then breaking its rules.

But then, that's what journalists sometimes have to do, he told himself, as he was shown out into the cold...

CONFIDENTIAL FILE

Fran Scott – her story 8
(transcribed from tape)

I don't know who this is for – Mum, Dad and Mikey, Gussie, the police, history, or me. Me, if I get out of this. (long pause) The news is, I've been to the loo and had a shower! Yes! And God, it makes a difference! The woman took me to a washroom – I don't know when, I live under electric light and I've got no watch so I don't know whether it's ten o'clock, eleven o'clock or Good Friday. I try to keep count by the meals, but my sleep pattern's all over the place, and what they give me isn't definitely a breakfast, a lunch, or a supper, they could be giving me whatever they've got, any time. But suddenly the door's unlocked, and with the man standing guarding it, the woman comes in and, big as a baths' attendant, she throws this bit of towel at me. It's a cut-off piece from a pull-down towel cabinet like we have in school, only this is the blue sort for manual workers. And she's got a scarf, a black one, and she starts winding it round my head and eyes.

'You want a shower, dirty girl?' she asks.

'Yeah – at my house!' I tell her. To which she says nothing but just jerks the scarf tight like a teacher who's got no kids, organising Blind Man's Buff at a Christmas party. Then she pushes me to the door.

The place smells a bit different outside the room. Could be I've got used to my own smell and the bucket inside, but there's definitely an oily, garagey smell out there. She holds my arms tight from behind and marches me forwards, twisting me to the left and straightening me up, going about twenty shuffling steps across or along this other place. I try to count the steps, but I forgot to do it from the start, so I'll do it next time. If there's a next time. What I do know is, these aeroplanes come over continually, two while I'm being pushed along, then I can hear a door thrown open and I'm twisted to the right, marched a couple more steps, and she leaves hold of me.

'Take the scarf off, I don' want it wet!' she says, 'an' I'll be back when I'm back.'

There's a locking of a door, and I untie the scarf. I'm in a gents' washroom! There are three urinals, a WC cubicle, a washbasin with a mirror on a cabinet, a radiator, and an open shower – just the spray nozzle coming out of the wall and a shower tray to stand in, no curtain. And a window! But it's crinkly glass with a grill outside it, and not much light – like an alley – and the small bit of the window that opens at the top is screwed so it only gives two inches. Anyhow, right then I'm not really taking any notice of anything except first things first! I've been dying to go to the lavatory all night long, holding on, holding on, trying not to use that bloody bucket again for more than a wee, and now I can, and I make it just in time. Blessed relief, and I'm sitting, not crouching. But, like with the bucket, there's paper there – and that shower in the corner!

I tell you, right now I don't care about the not having a shower curtain. Let the man look through the keyhole if he likes, I don't care. I just don't care; I'm sweaty, and stale, and dying for this. So I start running the shower and strip off. It's simple to use – two taps, a rubber hose, and the nozzle. And the water comes out hot, and, oh, it's heaven! I get the temperature right and stand under it, and with a bit of streaky soap reached from the washbasin I let the water wash me away.

And now, with the wet hair, wet face, wet body, I can't help but start to cry out my own wet – eyes, nose, dribble; I break my heart under that running water. Because I want to go home! I don't want to be here, I want to be where I can be too long in the bathroom and ticked off by my mum, and aggravated by Mikey, and have a good row with Dad about his policies. I want to be sent to bed, grounded, fed on bread and water, get a permanent detention at school and have to take Williams a cup of tea every breaktime and call her ma'am; I want to be where I can curtsey to one of the royals, even the dogs – but I want to be out of here! You get the picture? (long pause) And when I've run Britain dry of water in that shower, I come out of it, dry myself on the blue strip of towel, and look around. Grizzle over. Be brave, Fran!

I'm clean – but there's no clean clothes, what sort of regime is this?! I have to put the Holloway stuff on again, reminding me that I'm a real prisoner here. See the performance I'd give old Kenny Richards next time! And I've got no toothbrush. I want a toothbrush. Kidnappers should give you a bit of warning before they snatch you! You can go without combs and brushes but you can't go without a toothbrush. I swill my mouth around in the sink and spit and spit and spit like I do in my cell to rid myself of that chemical rag, and I look at myself in the mirror.

The stage make-up has run, my hair's a mess – but in the mirror I surprise myself: I'm quite beautiful in a gaunt, dying heroine sort of way. My eyes are big and tragic, that's what it is – but a comb through the hair wouldn't hurt. And as I look at the mirror above the sink, I realise that the mirror is on a cabinet. There's a cabinet here, and cabinets hold things!

Now I do care about the door to the washroom. Now I do

go over and hang my strip of towel on the door handle, covering the keyhole. And I rush back to look inside the cabinet.

And, first off, it's clear I'm not on suicide watch like some of the Holloway women – because in here there's a disposable razor and a bottle of pills, as well as a comb, their toothbrushes (erk!), toothpaste, and a small pack of Tampax. So, how professional are these people? Shouldn't they have cleared this stuff before I came in, because I could easily slit my wrist or down a bottle of paracetamol. Or don't they care what really happens to me? Am I just their bargaining chip, and I might come out of this alive or I might not, it's all the same to them?

But, you see, it isn't paracetamol! No! You know what it is – it's Mysoline! It's the white tablets with the line down the middle and the two little 'M's on it. They're what Mikey takes, for epilepsy.

So one of them's an epileptic!

Which is when she comes back. No knocking, she pushes straight into the washroom to grab up the scarf, him guarding the door again, and I just get a glimpse of what's behind him. A corridor, with breezeblocks, like the rest of the place. But just before it goes dark under the scarf I get a quick look at the man, only his eyes, of course, but I see a look in them that isn't a bit as hard as the look in hers. And it could have been a blink, but I think he winked at me, as if it's him who's got me this privilege. Well, well…

(tape clicks off)

ZEPHON TELEVISION

Transcript of voice-mail message

BEN MADDOX – MOBILE

Monday 21 October 09.30

Hi Ben! Bloom. Listen, Sherlock Homes, I've been standing outside this school for an hour and a quarter. I was here when the first parents arrived and I'm here after the last parents have left, even the late ones who had to ring the bell at the playground gate. And no one like Caitlin Jones has dropped anyone off, car or taxi – and there's been a few of those, there's money here – and no one looking like the file photograph of Michael Scott has been brought in by anyone else, detective, nursemaid, or next-door neighbour. He's not in school today, I'm certain of that. I thought of checking with one of the other kids but I'd have looked a perv, already I was getting the eye. Sorry! Anyhow, I'm going back to the office.

See ya! Bye!

Ends.

DOWNING STREET SW1

Ben tried to keep an unimpressed look on his face as he went through police security at the Horse Guards Road back entrance to Downing Street. He was with the best of the world's media for the Prime Minister's regular press briefing, and he didn't want to look the new boy. Bill Finch certainly wasn't a novice, neither was Jonny Aaranovitch, both with Ben in the Zephon car as it was let through the barrier after a careful scrutiny of press passes. There wasn't a lot of parking space up behind Number 10, so Zephon, from just across Waterloo Bridge, had got there early.

The famous mirror-black front door opened for them as they arrived, and they walked into the lobby, where, taking his cue from Finch and Aaronovitch, Ben left his mobile phone on the big sideboard, with a signed Post-it attached so that he got the right one back. Then it was through the cloakroom area and into the reception room where other crews were setting up – whose television floods meant that Jonny could travel light, hand held.

Bill Finch told Ben where to sit, next to him on the aisle four rows back, while Jonny took up a place standing down the side between the stepladders and Homebase plastic stools of those who preferred height to mobility.

Jonny was always good to be with, Ben and he had got on really well on the Magayana trip, and Finch was OK, Ben reckoned: not razor sharp, like Len Wyatt had been, nor with the expert air of a Jon Snow or Andrew Marr, but more a burrowing sort of creature who dug at things, could make a devastating question sound like an invitation to tea, and to whom politicians always listened very carefully when he interviewed them. Today he was Ben's mentor, asked to bring him along for the experience, look and learn.

Quickly, the big room filled up. Long windows with drapes drawn closed, a raised podium and an oak panelled door as background, provided the Prime Minister's setting. And it *was* a bit like waiting for a star performance. Looking around, a nervous sort of excitement ran in Ben's stomach, partly because of where he was: well-known faces, reporters, correspondents, and feature writers talking to each other, joking, sharing information, some talking to themselves down into dictaphones and cassettes. But the real source of Ben's nervousness came from what he might just be mad enough to do.

No one seemed to have seen Ben's interview with the Home Secretary, nobody said, 'Bad luck!' or 'That's the way it goes, boy!' Everyone was there for the Prime Minister. And it was while Ben was looking at his notes that the room suddenly went quiet, and when he looked up, there was the man himself at the podium. It was as if he had been beamed in: taller than Ben had imagined, wearing make up for the lights (his high aristocratic forehead matt and the lips red), and looking round with the confidence of a householder in his own living room. And there was definitely a star quality about him. This man ran the country, this man was the President of UK plc. His voice, as he said, 'Good morning!' was so familiar, and like being at a concert when the long awaited top of the bill comes on stage, Ben felt a new rush of excitement, nerves, and lack of oxygen.

But, quickly, a routine took over. Correspondents whose newspapers and media channels supported the government asked questions on those policies where the PM was definitely on top in the House of Commons – on grammar schools, private health care, and tough immigration controls for migrant workers. Those whose media owners opposed the government asked questions on university provision, equality of opportunity, and public transport, all very predictable stuff, and Ben might have switched off were it not for the fizz in his stomach and the uncertainty of his bowel brought on by the intention in his head.

It was Peter White of Channel Four News who suddenly got the cameras flashing, the tapes running, and the spiral notebook pages flicking over and over.

'Prime Minister,' he asked, 'would you say that this government has a moral dimension?'

'I don't follow, Peter,' answered the PM.

'Well, is this government giving a lead – in its own behaviour and the behaviour of its members – to the youth of this country? Are you all setting a good example?'

If there can be a silent flurry, it happened then. Intakes of breath, when there are enough of them, can stir the air. Journalists had commented on the Prime Minister two-timing his wife but no one had asked the man a direct question about it: everyone was waiting for it to cost him at the next election.

The Prime Minister leant forward on the podium. 'The day your government members, or your opposition members, are not human beings will be the day when rigid fascist control takes over,' he said.

'Do you feel impelled to resign, Prime Minister?' White followed up.

But the PM lifted his nose in the air at a suggestion so far beneath contempt. *Any other sensible questions?* his eyes asked, deliberately not White's way.

Bill Finch swore softly. 'Bugger's nicked my line!' Ben knew that Kate Lewis and Finch had another 'royal and politician indiscretion' package ready for tonight's ten o'clock bulletin, the scandal was coming to a head. But he doubted if Bill would actually have been so bold.

Which was when Ben suddenly heard his own voice breaking a short but definite silence. 'Ben Maddox, Zephon News,' he said.

The PM looked at him, a slight frown, as if he were wondering who this was; this young man had never been on his plane, in his train, in the Commons lobby; he wouldn't know where he was coming from; yet the snoot of the PM's nose suggested that he might have seen Dennis Scott make mincemeat of him the previous Thursday. 'Yes?' he pointed.

'Why is the government fabricating evidence against Claude Chaumet to get him deported to Magayana where he faces execution?' Those words, the phrasing of the question, had been running round and round in Ben's head since he woke; he was surprised he hadn't said them in the car. Now they were out in the open.

There was a groan from some of the old hands; Zephon's obsession with Chaumet was becoming a bore.

'No, no,' said the PM, quietening the groans with a conductor's hands. 'This is intriguing. Let me say first that Magayana is a friendly state to whom we owe a lot. They fought alongside us in several conflicts, and they will be seen to be a great friend to us in the future.' Here he allowed himself a small smile and a nod of great confidence; anticipation, almost. 'As to fabricating evidence for the deportation of a minority figure who has failed to meet the high standards of international life, I am sure any such claims will be dealt with in the ongoing appeal.' And he pointed to Sue Verity of the 'Telegraph' at the back of the room for the next question, which was on union legislation.

No one much looked at Ben. No one spoke to him. It took Bill Finch all the time to get back to their car before he said anything. 'That came out of the blue!' he said. 'Did Kath

Lewis put you up to it?' He wasn't pleased.

'No. It's *my* top line at the moment.'

'Clearly. Well, a word to the wise: senior colleagues expect to be in the loop, OK?' And that was all.

Jonny Aaranovitch also said nothing, but he hummed to himself all the way back to Zephon; and, when Bill Finch had gone off to moan to Kath Lewis, he took Ben to a tape machine and showed him his footage, stopping the frame where the PM had smiled in the middle of his answer to Ben.

'See that?' he said. 'If we were a newspaper I'd run that on the front page. You ask me what my caption would be?' He looked at Ben in triumph. '"The Magayana Smile"!'

'How do you mean?'

'That was the moment, wasn't it? All you want to know, it tells you. He needs Magayana to keep him in Number Ten, and he thinks he's got it. All over his face, it's written!'

'You think so?'

'Shut up with a homily, that was Peter White, "let him who casts the first stone", and so on. But he knows, the shyster! It will cost him at the next election, his sordid little affair, unless it's some victorious war he pulls off, or an economic miracle. And this he thinks he's got!'

'As serious as that?' Ben asked.

'The features, look at them! The only time he smiled in the whole briefing.'

There it was, sure enough, the confident glint of a soon-to-come win, an historic smile on the rouged, unfaithful lips. 'He thinks some Magayanan mineral will save his political life.'

Ben stared at Jonny's certain face; and he was suddenly more proud than ever to be a probing journalist on the case. To keep digging, as Claude Chaumet had asked.

Fran Scott – her story 9
(transcribed from tape)

After the shower, they come in with some food, and a small plastic table and a garden chair. Up to now I've sat or lain on the mattress, or stood up and leaned. My first thought is, good, I'm pleased, this'll be more comfortable; but my second thought is, hell! – home improvements, this means I'm here for a long time. A shower, use of a proper lavatory, now this... He brings the furniture and she brings the food – a slice of warmed-through take-away pizza, an apple, and a glass of Coke, puts them on the table like they're a treat. But she's been looking around the cell as if I'm hiding a boyfriend or something.

'What more does anyone want?' she says through her balaclava, as if she expects me to thank them. But why should I thank them for anything, when they've put me into this situation, when they might do what they still might do...?

Except, a shower is better than the sink, a lavatory is better than the bucket, and a table and chair is better than the floor. So I thank them; just a quick, 'Ta.'

She's in a different dress – Marks and Spencer's from last summer. Is she going off somewhere, dressed like that? I think she might be, because she doesn't stay, she takes out the bowl I'd had some pasta in before – picks it up off the floor as if I'm a dog – and out she goes. He stands in the doorway, the door still unlocked, and I wonder what my chances would be if I tried to take him and get through that door – but not good, I reckon. No, not good. He's muscly as if he works out, and because of the mission he's on, he wouldn't hold back from getting rough. Besides, I don't know that the woman's not just round the corner, outside.

He's got his eyes half closed like someone thinking about something else, and I start to wonder if he did take a look through that washroom keyhole. Is he having a little moment, standing there staring at me again? But he suddenly says, 'Saw your play, girl. You are one half-good actress.'

'I was superb!' I splutter back at him, a mouthful of pizza. The stinking cheek!

'Is what I mean. You were good. Good at givin' off that you're a prisoner.'

'Practice for this, then, wasn't it?!' I snort.

'Older. A woman, more.'

Oh, come on! I draw back a bit from the table, give myself room to move. Is this where he's going? If he's coming on about me being a woman I suddenly start seeing myself using the chair like a lion tamer, the legs in his face.

'Yeah, really good.' He was still looking me up and down.

'Write down your thoughts and I'll stick it in my scrapbook.' The creep! I stand up; hot pizza, cold pizza, what difference? He's got a weird, embarrassed hang to his body, the sort Mikey has when he's thinking of getting up to something. And the thought of Mikey almost makes me play a dodgy card.

I almost ask him, 'Is it grand mal, petit mal, or partial? Your illness?' Just to see the reaction: sort, of, think about that instead, Sunshine! But I don't, because the less I know about these people – the less they know I know – then the more chances I've got of getting out of this alive. All the same, I wonder if I can't use what I know somehow...

But I do want to do something, not be passive, I want to play on him a bit. I hate being in a room alone with a man like this, but I reckon I could let him get in my good books. So I suddenly say, 'You want to do me a favour?'

'What favour?' He's interested.

'Fresh clothes,' I say. I really mean fresh underwear, but I'm not going into that with him. 'And I'm going mad in here. I've got nothing to do except be scared of you two coming in! That cassette recorder, have you got any music for it?'

He purses his lips, thinking. 'Could have,' he says.

'And books, or a book. Could you get me something to read? Please?'

He goes on looking. 'I'll give myself a think,' he says.

'Don't burst a blood vessel!'

And suddenly he laughs; but quietly, a chuckle just for our room. 'You got spirit, girl!' he tells me. 'You got spirit the same I had, the same as my blessed mother...'

'She's not your mother?'

And I could have just cracked the joke of the century. He doubles over laughing, hugging himself, his eyes actually start crying with the laugh he's having. 'No, she's not my mother.' And he sobers up in a flick of his fingers. 'She's dead, my mother, God rest her. She died, in prison, under torture, in a nearby cell to where I had all the spirit like you...' And suddenly I knew the tears were not part of the laughing, they were part of the sadness. He opens his mouth to say some more.

But, 'Don't tell me about it!' I warn him. 'I don't want to know. I mustn't know. The less I know about you the better.' I start poking myself in the chest. 'I'm hung out to dry enough as it is.'

'I'll just tell you, I was thinking of her an' I was thinking of me when I saw your play. Is all. That's how I know you are good.'

I stand looking at him, arms by my side, thinking of it. The pizza's going hard and the Coke's losing its fizz, but I have to take some moments getting my head round what this man's about.

There's a long, long silence – if you can count it as silence with low, heavy aircraft going over all the time, the sounds of traffic somewhere, and now, much nearer, the rattle of a roller door going down or up.

'I'll get you some music,' he says. 'Yeah, I will.' And he goes, leaving me to wonder how the hell I played all that. Did I do myself any good, or what? (long pause) I reckon you'll know by now...

(tape clicks)

HOUSE OF COMMONS
LONDON SW1 0AA

OFFICE OF THE PRIME MINISTER

CABINET LEVEL MINUTES – TOP SECRET

Meeting between the Prime Minister and the Rt. Hon. Dennis Scott MP, Secretary of State for Home Affairs: Tuesday, 22nd October at 11 am.

Present: In addition to the Prime Minister and the Home Secretary there were present: Sir Nigel Craddock, Home Office Advisor; Dame Jhyoti Riat Kaur, Senior Cabinet Officer; Mrs Pauline Allen, minuter.

Agenda: One item only: the Deportation Appeal to the Home Office of Claude Chaumet, leader of the People's Democratic Party of Magayana, resident at 33, Westcombe Park Drive, London SE3 8ER.

Sir Nigel Craddock briefly outlined the background to the Appeal, that the original Deportation Order arose from Mr Chaumet's flouting of residency conditions for foreign politicians; namely that they should abide by the laws of this country with regard to road traffic acts, local parking byelaws, and the non-use of residential properties for political meetings and rallies. Mr Chaumet had not abided by the agreed code of conduct and was, conditional upon the outcome of any appeal, to be deported from the UK at the end of the fourteen days allowed.

Sir Nigel went on to read the basis of Mr Chaumet's appeal; namely, that he had not transgressed any of the traffic act or byelaws as stated, and that he had not held meetings at his residence with more than six people at a time. His meetings and rallies had all been held in public halls for the hire of which he appended receipts. Mr Chaumet went on to accuse the president of Magayana, President Jorge Gomez, of waging economic and ethnic warfare, and of being guilty of seeking to create a similar situation in his own country to that of Bosnia in the 1990s.

Dame Jhyoti Riat Kaur, acting as 'devil's advocate', stated that in her, admittedly skimmed reading of the documents, Mr Chaumet appeared to have made a good case for the upholding of his Appeal. On the face of it, he should not be deported since the local charges would not have 'stuck' for an ordinary citizen, a view that sections of the media would support, and allowing the Appeal would be an action that the British public would support.

The Prime Minister reminded those present that the meeting was Top Secret and that his ensuing comments were not to be leaked, briefed upon, nor the subject of private conversations with other Members of Parliament. Reasons for failing an appeal in a case like this could be said to fall under the Official Secrets Act and not be given.

Claude Chaumet was a danger to the economic well-being of Great Britain since his attempted pursuance of the intervention of the United Nations in the situation in Magayana could lead to the sugar plantation owners being allowed to cultivate their crops. Any legal action inside Magayana would slow the exploitation of the mineral SQ1 and would allow other neighbouring states – with stronger affiliations to the USA – to search for, and possibly find, deposits of SQ1. This would seriously weaken the United Kingdom's hoped-for lead in the industry concerned.

There was some debate about the ethical stance being taken by Her Majesty's Government, in which the <u>Secretary of State for Home Affairs the Rt. Hon. Dennis Scott</u> reminded the meeting of the Home Office credo, to build a 'safe, just and tolerant society'. He was inclined to support the upholding of the Appeal, and in favour of making an early public announcement that Mr Chaumet should be freed from house arrest and allowed to continue his normal activities. He also cited the opinion that in being returned to Magayana, Mr

Chaumet faced serious consequences, including the possibility of execution.

The Prime Minister, however, told the meeting that the greater good for Great Britain, for generations to come, would be better served by Mr Chaumet's deportation. When this deportation was a matter of history, and forgotten by the media and the electorate, the spectacular economic gains for the country would result in huge popularity for the Parliamentary Party, and would put into insignificance the current local difficulty over personal affairs that he, the Prime Minister, was having. The Appeal should be dismissed.

Mr Dennis Scott and Sir Nigel Craddock bowed to this view, but **Mr Scott** pointed out that he would prefer that no decision be announced prematurely, and that the meeting should be cognisant of the fact that circumstances could always change.

The meeting ended at 11.23 am.

Ben was searching on the world wide web at his kitchen desk. Meera had gone early to bed with Caitlin Jones's *Nelly Mabel Powell*, just in case she ever had to pretend to interview her on Ben's behalf. But she wasn't really into the book and she quickly came out of Chapter One at the sound of a low 'Yes!' from the kitchen.

'What?' She ran from the bedroom.

Ben turned the laptop so that she could see. He was on a page of results for drilling companies, reached by asking for a Drilling Directory. 'Look at that,' he said.

EXCITE Web Search

Results for Drilling Directory

1. **Birch Lake Project**
   Mineral exploration project to determine the presence of platinum group metals.
2. **Birch Mountain Resources Ltd.**
   M.e.p. to determine the presence of platinum group metals.
3. **Calista Corporation**
   Regional corporation, Alaska – oil and gas exploration and mining for gold, silver, platinum and mercury.
4. **Explo-Mine Ltd**
   Exploration and small mining of heavy mineral deposits.
   Specialist in sub-Saharan Africa.
5. **Freed (Robert) – GB Ltd.**
   Mineral exploration company for new mining.
   South American geological specialism.

6. **Major General Resources Ltd.**
   Mineral exploration of diamond, gold and base metal deposits.
7. **PC Exploration**
   A drilling services contractor.
8. **Uravan Minerals Inc.**
   Mining and exploration contracting company.
   Staking, prospecting, geochemical sampling, geological mapping and line cutting.

'There!' Ben said. 'Concentrate on number five.'

Meera looked over his shoulder. 'Robert Freed?'

'"GB". Great Britain.'

'I know what GB means.'

'And South America…'

'"And South America."'

'The only one. So, now look at what we find at Robert Freed (GB) Limited.' Ben swiftly fingered the laptop to the Robert Freed website. And there, with all the commercial puffs and links to the marvellous drilling that Robert Freed did, with glossy photographs of the chairman and a couple of top dogs, was a picture of a hard working drilling crew at what they called an appraisal site, somewhere unidentified.

'A drilling rig,' Meera said, 'a derrick – what you'd expect, Brains?'

'Thank you. But look at the background of the picture. What's that, all along the skyline?'

Meera fished her glasses from the pocket of her dressing gown and peered at the computer image. 'Smoke,' she said, 'a big fire of some sort…'

'Right. Very big. Miles long – smoke, smoke, smoke, smoke, smoke. And is anyone in the picture bothered about it?'

'The drilling crew?' Meera gave Ben a look, then stared at the image again. 'All happy little workers,' she said.

Ben nodded. 'So to them the smoke is nothing remarkable. It's part of the landscape at whatever time this picture was taken... Now where could that be?' He gave Meera a chance to come up with the answer, a slightly cocky edge to his face.

'Burning off the foliage from the sugar cane,' she said, 'prior to cutting.'

'Exactly. That's what I think.'

'So?'

'So it points to which of the main drilling companies has done some appraisal drilling in a sugar producing country – Robert Freed GB, and probably not a million miles from Magayana...' Ben sat back. 'There's nothing more on the website, but it's enough to give us a lead.' He rubbed his hands. 'We're getting somewhere! It could help Chaumet...'

'It could help Zephon.'

Ben ignored the dig; journalists got them all the time, questioning their integrity. 'If only we could get into Robert Freed's files and drilling reports...'

'Or if only we could get at one of his workers,' Meera added – with a nice line in smug on her own face. 'Nice hunky looking fellows. Well done, Maddox.'

'Yes,' he said, nodding vigorously, 'good idea – thanks! But the intention isn't always the deed.'

Meera smiled. 'It could be,' she said, 'like, right now, young Ben. Come to bed. I'm not as engrossed by *Nelly Mabel Powell* as you are by your laptop.'

'I'm sorry to hear that,' Ben sympathised. But he shut the laptop down for the evening, anyway.

VICTORIA SW1

In shirt and braces, Dennis Scott sat with a very large scotch, definitely no water, and faced a sheet of white paper. He faced it, and faced it, and refilled his glass – and finally, he unscrewed the cap of the Waterman's pen that Fran and Michael had bought him last birthday, and started to write.

Meeting with P.M a disaster: but held off from having to deport Chaumet here and now.

Thoughts:
Have done –
Ready for their next contact, have set up a 'track and trace' operation for incoming telephone calls on all lines, inc. mobile. Can then get back to them and offer them a deal.
Also, have asked for a list of all known Magayanan citizens currently in the UK. Useful for Krol, if Krol is employed.
Will do –
Must make crystal clear to these terrorists that while I am the one to deport C – constitutionally it's got to be my signature on the document, not the Queen's, not the bloody P.M's – I can't do the opposite, let him stay, without losing us the Mag. deal and bringing down the P.M and the govt.
Could do –
Call their bluff and go public – set the bloodhounds on them. How very wise would that be? Bluffing with Fran's life? Don't think so!
What's the deal to offer? –
If they release Fran, I'll persuade the Overseas Development people to pour big scale government aid to help compensate the M. sugar growers. Surely, this is what they want.

Bottom line –

The PM's mad driven on Magayana to save himself and the party. If I don't deport Chaumet, he'll quietly have some nasty accident happen to him anyway, prob. trying to escape, which will all be too late for Fran.

He read it over, folded it, and slipped it into his pocket – and like everybody who ever waited for a telephone call, he looked again at his glowing mobile, reached over again to check that the landline phone was safely on its rest; actions that he did these days as regularly as blinking his eyelids.

HOUNSLOW, MIDDLESEX

It was pouring with rain outside, a chilly October evening. The Heathrow aeroplanes sounded even heavier than usual as they got in under the low clouds, and the radiator in the office space where Laurina Modeste and Augustin Baptiste had their mattresses was turned up full. It was the first of those nights in the autumn when staying indoors is preferable to going out. They sat on swivel office chairs watching a dusty portable television, every news bulletin monitored in case word of Claude Chaumet came out. They had strict instructions not to make further contact with D, he would ring them; every phone call held its dangers; so their first indication that the kidnap was working could be an announcement that Chaumet would be allowed to stay. In reality, though, they knew they might have to wait until the appeal period was up – and this could be just the start of the long drag of being hostage takers.

Baptiste finished the plate of ready-prepared curry that

he'd heated through, wiped it off with pitta bread and slid it onto the desk where the TV sat. He nodded at the latest news in the Prime Minister scandal, shots of the girlfriend through long lens cameras, hiding somewhere in the country.

'So, where's the boy, this...Michael?' he asked Laurina. He dropped his voice on the name. 'Still in the house?'

'Not at school today, anyhow,' she muttered, her own curry pushed aside in favour of a cigarette. 'I'll go checkin' past the place tomorrow. An' if D gets a sniff of where he is, he'll text us. He'll be tracking relations—' And she suddenly stopped. 'What's the hell's that?' she asked, up out of her chair.

It was loud music, coming from the room along the corridor.

Laurina swore. 'That's my 'Retha Franklin!'

'Calm yourself! I let the girl have it,' Baptiste told her, 'an' a few others. Stop her going mad. Helps us, uh? And she needs some books, fresh clothes, too...'

'Does she?' Laurina looked at him with contempt. 'So is she talkin' to you, askin' you little favours when I'm out, big man?'

'There can't be harm in treating her decent till I do what I might have to do. Maybe.' He reached over to finish Laurina's curry. 'You have clothes stuff she can have...'

'Yeah? Same size as me anywhere, is she? Are you noticin'?' Laurina pushed herself out at him, all her forty inches.

Baptiste slammed down the plate. 'Not noticing! Not that way!'

Laurina stared into his eyes. 'I'm thinkin' you're not *any* way! Dear Jesus in heaven, not any way normal!' But, after a long pause, lowering her voice, she stubbed out her cigarette and put a hand on his shoulder. 'It's a cold, wet night, man, and here's a challenge for you – what if we make those two mattresses into one? Uh?' And her hand went to the top button of his shirt. 'What does our big man think about that?'

'No!' he said quickly, pushing her hand away. 'Keep yourself cool. I'm on a mission here!'

Laurina's sneer had the angry contempt of every person ever insulted by a refusal. 'Yeah!' she said. 'Yeah! How did I know you wouldn't be up to it?' – before grabbing her coat from the hook on the door and throwing it round herself. 'I'm goin' out! To eat somethin' decent instead of that shit, an' to drink somethin' good an' harder than coca.'

With which she slammed out of the office, and the next thing heard by Baptiste was the sound of the roller shutter being thrown up.

In the street Laurina angrily pulled down on the shutter to close it, swore again, up into the sky at a 747, covered her head against the heavy rain with her hood, and ran off up the street to get away from the industrial estate and find the Indian restaurant in Packer Row where a real curry would be on the menu.

But she left behind her a roller shutter that had not quite made it to the ground, and a homeless young man with a homeless old dog who found it – a drier place than the doorway they'd been in – and who slid themselves inside to lie and wait for the rain to stop.

CONFIDENTIAL FILE

Fran Scott – her story 10
(transcribed from tape)

He knocks on the door the next time. I jump up and back over against the wall. I jump up and back over against the wall every time because every time it could be the last! What's he coming for, an empty curry plate? Or to do something drastic to me? But when he lets himself in he's got another couple of cassettes in his hand, and a book, a bent and scruffed copy of Easy Rawnsley Brown. *So, his book, I reckon, not hers.*

'Brought you these, too,' he says, dismissive. He throws them down on the mattress. And from out of his jeans pocket he pulls a pair of grey knickers. 'And them.' But he won't look at them, which is a bit of a good sign.

'Cheers. Now I can be decent when they find me.' But if I think a remark like that is going to give me any hope through seeing his reaction, I'm badly disappointed.

'Well, I'll leave you to—' He flaps his hand at the pants on the mattress.

'Tomorrow. When I've had my shower,' I tell him.

So he perches on the edge of the garden table looking at his hands; he doesn't want to go. I turn off the Aretha Franklin – I only had it on loud so they knew I was playing it, using the cassette recorder for the purpose he thought.

'Yeah, prison…' he says. 'Back home.'

'I told you, I don't want to know!' I tell him. 'I don't want to know anything about you!' And, taking the cassettes and book from him it hits me all over again in a great churning wave of fear – never mind the hidden face, I know those eyes

so well, I can describe the scar on his arm, I know he's missing half a little finger. I can pick him out if ever I get out of here, and he must know that. Which means he doesn't care about any of that. Which could mean I am not meant to survive! And, God help me, I start to cry. I tell him, 'I don't want…any more reason for you to…do anything to me…than you've already got!' I pull myself together and sit down. 'What I don't know I can't let on to anyone.'

He shifts his backside, uncomfortable: but his eyes looking at me tell me that he might just have to do something terrible to me… Holding back, pinprick pupils, like Dad when he's deliberately not telling us a government secret. And a mad thought comes again, a crazy idea I'd had curled up on that mattress. What if I could rile him up to where he has a fit, if it's him who's the epileptic and not her? It's happened to Mikey, by accident: but what if I did it deliberately? Because, supposing it's him? How controlled is his illness? Is he on the right dose? And anyone's anti-convulsant balance can be upset by stress. Also, I know the woman's out, I'd heard that roller shutter sound again – and he never comes in like this when she's around, wanting to talk.

And he's got the key to my cell in his pocket…

But he's too controlled, sitting there as still as an art lesson model. How could I stress him?

'When a people's real downtrodden no one knows how bad it is,' he says, all quiet in his throat. He's going to tell me: I'm his prisoner and he won't shut up, I'm going to have to listen. 'Some tribal things, yeah – Zimbabwe, Saddam Hussein's Iraq and the Kurds, the old apartheid South Africa, people knew all about that…'

I sit in the chair and ball myself up as tight as I can. I fold my arms. I set my face as closed as it can get without my eyes shut. I'm not open to all this.

'...But some countries look as if they're running along fine. To the rest of the world. OK, two sets of peoples, some tribal strife, a few social problems and criminal stuff – like Guyana – but to the rest of the world it's nothin'. Nothin'! Friendly country, no problem! Turn the blind eye.' He screws up his forehead as if he's remembering; pulling out some terrible pictures behind those eyes: I know he is; he's anguished. 'You never see inside the prisons, though. You don't know in the outside world who's taken, who's tortured, who's disappeared, who's living, who's dead. Diplomats bow and scrape in London and Paris and New York – the same time as terrible things are going on back home, one people against another – and these men and women who kiss the queen's hand have blood coagulating on their own. My mother's, rest her. My father's in front of her. And some pints of mine.' And he shoves his hands in his pockets.

He wriggles his body, and I cough, sort of, clearing my throat of his memories: because some sound is called for.

'So in putting some of this straight, in bringing this to the attention of the blind world—'

Yes? Yes? I'm crying out to say, because I know he's getting round to me. He's swivelling on that table, and he's coming back from wherever he's been in his head.

'—So one politician's daughter in the scheme of things is not such a dreadful sacrifice. Not to someone like me.'

God! "Sacrifice!" That word suddenly sinks you like the great hand of death! That word when you hear it is the biggest concrete block for weighting you down you could ever hear! A cold skin of ice freezes across me, my lips start trembling, my arms roughen up like grit, my legs start shaking. Sacrifice!

'What if I'm...on your side?' I finally get out. 'What if I think you're in the right? I could! Sounds like it. I'm in Amnesty International.'

He just shrugs, and gets up. 'Anyhow, we're praying it won't come to that,' he says. And he waves his hand lightly like a substitute for a smile, something looking genuine when you're living on the thinnest wedge of hope. 'Lookin' good,' he says, 'hoping it won't.'

When suddenly there's this almighty scream from outside – a scream of shock and anger. The woman! Really out of her pram! I know it's the woman, she's always got a scream in her voice. And she suddenly shouts out loud with a word I definitely don't want to hear. 'Baptiste!' she yells.

She gives me his name! He runs to the door, unlocks it, gets himself out, locks up again. And that's another nail in my coffin: knowing that name. All this time there's shouting out there from someone else, some other voice: a man, rough and angry, shouting abuse. And when Baptiste gets to him – and I hear him shouting, too, 'Get out of here! Get out!' – there's the sounds of a fight, and a dog barking, and the roller shutter being hit as if there's something bashing against it; and then the shutter goes up and comes down, and a God Almighty row goes on between the two of them. My warders, my executioners, shouting on at each other about security.

And I put out the light and curl up small on my mattress and lie there in terror, crying into those clean knickers, and wondering how they're going to kill me when it comes to it...

(tape clicks)

WATERLOO STATION, LONDON SE1

The following morning Ben stood on the station concourse between commuter Platform One and the Underground, causing a tide of passengers to swirl around him like angry water. But he neither minded nor even noticed that; he was too engrossed in the piece he was reading from the latest edition of *Drilling World,* just bought from WH Smith's.

REEL HARD WORK

The Robert Freed boys are acting the part these days. Instead of drilling for real they're drilling for 'reel' – reels of 35 mm celluloid for a new Anthony Jordan film being shot in the flat Essex marshes, standing in for a Brazilian swamp.

Jordan told us, 'You can't fake an appraisal derrick out of polystyrene so we've gone for the real thing. But my contract says that if they find anything down there, I'm in for ten per cent!'

Nice work if you can get it!

Well! And Ben apologised to himself for the unintended pun; but Meera had been right – and this piece meant that it might be possible to get to some Robert Freed workers. And there was always the chance that one of them had worked in

Magayana, or that they knew someone who had – it was a miles better chance of finding out what they'd been drilling for out there than trying to hack into the secret files of the Freed office. And, what luck – this crew wasn't sweating over oil in Nova Scotia, it was on a jolly not far from London, where they'd be as laid back as duvets on a film set, being pampered, eating location catering, chatting up the famous faces – and, as he thought of it, who else was good at that? Whose speciality was showbiz, who Ben knew and trusted; who might tempt a hardened crewman into a few loose words, if anyone could? The beautiful Bloom Ramsaram. And who should be the cameraman with her, someone who was well in the Magayana loop? Jonny Aaranovitch. Apart from himself, they were the dream team – and he wanted to follow up on the Frances Scott mystery.

All of which was digging, wasn't it, making the luck? That's what Kath Lewis wanted – and the result of it all could very much be what Claude Chaumet wanted, too.

Ben folded the *Drilling World* into his shoulder bag to fight his way across the tide and out to the Waterloo Road, to make his pitch to Kath Lewis for a day of Bloom's and Jonny's time – still unaware of the turbulence he was causing around him.

KENSINGTON W8

Legwork.

After the nod from Kath Lewis, Ben headed by tube for Kensington High Street. It was a blustery October lunchtime. Through the newly painted blue and gold school gates Ben saw into the grounds of Kensington Girls' High School, where younger pupils were running about like blown crisp bags while the older girls stood huddled under archways and behind pillars, eating sandwiches, drinking Coke, talking and screeching at gusty gossip. He was looking for the girl he'd met in Kensington Mews, Frances Scott's friend, but there was no sign of her. Above him, he saw the slow nod and sweep of a school CCTV camera and he realised that he had to look a real perv, standing here watching the schoolgirls, so he went on into the grounds. Being the lunch hour, the gate gave without any problem and he walked towards the reception area as if he had an appointment.

Walking up and down Lippard Street, tying in the street CCTV images he'd seen with the reality on the pavement, he'd wondered about who had been in the audience that first night of the play – parents, friends, official visitors, and who else? Did the school have a guest list, and would they release it to a reporter who was pretending he was researching parental support for out-of-school activities around the country? While on the royalist front, were some people disappointed not to get tickets that night to see Princess Anne? – meaning, how popular was the royal family? These were the questions he could ask, although he suspected the sort of blocking he would get; but then you don't win the lottery unless you buy a ticket, so he pressed the buzzer on the entry key pad at the school door and told them who he was.

'Ben Maddox, Zephon TV,' he said, 'to see Mrs Wellington.'

There was a lengthy pause for thought, then the door clicked, and with a push it gave, and he was in the reception area. He ignored two sick girls dressed for home sitting on the reception sofa, and the teachers busying about and the short queue of girls outside the head's door – and they all ignored him. But the secretary/receptionist was watching him keenly from her doorway so he made for her with a pleasant smile, not overdone. As he approached he saw behind her in the office an excellent quality colour CCTV monitor of the school gate. He was on the record.

'I wondered if—'

'Mr Maddox, Mrs Wellington's busy, you don't have an appointment, and she's teaching all afternoon. Can I help?' The headteacher's protector was tall and ladylike, about fifty, with the satisfied face of someone who has a regular seat at the Royal Festival Hall.

'It's about—'

'What you wanted last week? The filming? I'm afraid that won't be possible, you really should have come back to us that afternoon. It's all been taken down.' She also had a good memory for names.

'No, it's—'

'Mr Richards isn't in today, anyway, and his drama deputy is running a club this lunch hour, and then he's in class till four o'clock.'

'What I wanted was—'

'If you make a proper appointment for Friday, I could give you the deputy headteacher for twenty minutes at eleven a.m....'

Ben did a full three-sixty degree turn, sort of, came in again, fresh start. This woman hadn't let him get a word out. He wanted to ask her if she fancied a quick snog on a PE mat, just to snap her mouth shut; but he kept his calm. 'I'm doing audience research,' he told her, fast.

'Audience research? In a school?'

'School audience. Who comes to school events these days? How is Sports Day supported? What numbers come to—'

'We don't do Sports Day here. Too competitive.'

'Well, Founder's Day, Speech Day, plays like last week's… Do people turn out the same as they used to in this television and DVD age?'

'If you ask your colleagues and friends who are parents pretty well anywhere I should have thought they'd tell you about all that…'

'Yes, but I want to flesh it out…'

The woman caught her breath at the word 'flesh'. He reckoned his PE mat suggestion would definitely have left her lost for words.

'Simple stuff. Statistical,' he persevered. 'Does the caretaker have to put out more chairs for governors' reports than for the carol service? Or don't you do God?' Ben finished. He was getting nowhere near to learning classified school information like the make-up of the play's audience – as he'd suspected he wouldn't, but it had been worth a chance. Then suddenly, out of nowhere, came a lead, like the first click of a security door being released.

'We don't do services, but for anything about chairs and seating you'd have to ask Mr Way.'

'Ah, Mr Way.'

'Our caretaker.'

'And where would I find him?'

The woman shrugged. A shrug that said she knew but wasn't prepared to say. 'He's off duty at present.' But Ben was already moving for the door with a quick thank you. Mr Way! From his own experience of school caretakers and university janitors, they all ran their own little kingdoms: academic staff members always either bought them off or ran scared of them. He should have thought of it earlier. A journalistic maxim he'd forgotten so far was *Always go for the caretaker!* And girls in a girls' school would know a male caretaker's habits and habitats, wouldn't they?

Outside the building, still under the secretary's watchful eye, Ben asked a group of girls, who weren't affronted at being spoken to by this pleasant young man.

'Excuse me...'

'Hi-ya!' they said.

'Mr Way? Caretaker. Where would I find him?'

The answer to the sort of place he could be found was obvious. Nowhere near them, thanks! Wide eyes and wrinkled noses told Ben he was a man who either stank or who fancied himself with the girls, a character to be watched, someone never to be alone with in a form-room.

'Right now he'll be in the pub,' one of them said, not even a look at a watch. 'Down on the corner. Can't miss him, gelled hair, eyes on the look-out, and a big...idea of himself.' Laughs and whoops.

'Cheers.'

'Mine's a Breezer!' another girl put in, as Ben turned away.

Ben gave her his straight *Mr Home Secretary*! look. 'Not till you've drunk up all your milk,' he told her: and went, to some mild abuse and a wolf whistle.

He found Mr Way without difficulty. He was the drinker who looked up before anyone else when Ben went in through the pub door. The girls were right – he was definitely a man on the look-out; shiny hair and a convenient seat next to him with a magazine minding it at his table for two. When he saw it was a man coming in he quickly looked back at the tabloid paper he was reading.

Ben went straight in, lifted the magazine off the reserved seat and put it on the table. It was a man's read: *What Makes Girls Blush?*

'Oi! That seat's—' Mr Way turned the magazine face down.

'Reserved, yes. I won't be a moment.' Ben sat down. 'Is it Mr Way?'

'Could be.'

'I'm Ben Maddox, Zephon Television.'

'Oh, yes?' The man's tone was a bit less aggressive; the word 'television' both excited people and put them on their guard.

Ben shook Way's hand, which had a smooth, silky feel, unusual for a caretaker who sometimes had to work manually. 'Mr Way, we're doing a documentary on the use of institutional closed circuit television. Schools, hospitals, that sort of thing, as opposed to shops and councils. Are they cost effective, are they reliable? A Zephon special. We want an interview with an expert, and your people at the school said you might be helpful.'

'Oh, yes?'

'They seemed to think you were the man to represent them. Telegenic face.' Ben let it sink in. 'Would you be prepared to be filmed? We pay generous appearance fees, you could probably name it.'

Mr Way obviously liked the prospect. He gave Ben a shot of his profile by looking towards the bar and back at him. 'Depends on several things,' he said, with a little flash of his white teeth.

'Ah, yes. What are you drinking?'

'Bitter, ta. Skinner's.'

Ben bought him one, and a pint for himself, came back to sit down, drawing his chair in closer. He'd appealed to vanity and to greed, and for Mr Way they were probably two of the three most important things in life.

'We'd look at a typical week, Mr Way—'

'Doug.'

'—Preferably last week, Doug, with the royal visit, so perhaps not so typical, but we'd look at your coverage, pixel out the faces, of course, but simply judge the quality of the recordings...' These, Ben knew, would be good; Mr Way would be proud to appear with such a high resolution product. 'Then what we'd want from you, straight interview to camera, would be a few facts about tape lengths, tape life, digital possibilities, and some costings. Could you get that information from the school office, or does your department have it?'

'Got it.' Said through a good gulp of bitter.

Liar! Ben thought, but Mr Way would be a man who would get hold of it. 'So can you leave things to a deputy back at the school while we run some tapes through? This afternoon? After your lunch hour?'

'That's no problem.'

'Great. Then why don't we have another wet while I talk fees and possible filming dates?' Ben took out his palm organiser, laid it on the table showing its Zephon TV home page, and went to fetch more drinks. He'd got Mr Way where he wanted him, he knew, and within half an hour they were in the Caretaker's Office – bigger than Ben's desk space at Zephon – with the blinds down and the tape running from the school gate camera. All the while, the caretaker talked endlessly about the CCTV system, sounding his t's, stilting his style so as not to sound like a caretaker, but Ben's concentration was all on the screen. He hardly blinked as he watched the audience filing in, the arrival of the local and government bigwigs, and the gush of people around HRH the Princess Royal when she drove up.

'Of course, we won't show Anne without Her Majesty's permission,' Ben interjected.

'Lucky we've kept that evening's tapes,' Doug Way put in. 'Actually, she's the reason.' As if that were surprising! 'One for the alcoves.'

'Who *wouldn't* keep it, Doug?'

Ben watched on, foot after foot after foot – until suddenly, blessed fortune, there it was! He almost missed it, had to rewind. But there, after an hour's tape time of a long gap with nothing happening, coming out of the school door, on their own, were the three figures that Ben had spotted from the council's Lippard Street camera. There was the same central figure, head down, feet almost dragging, a black finger-nailed hand round the neck of one of the others. And there were the other two, not seen from the back as they'd been in the street, but here in the school grounds seen from the front.

'What's this?' Ben asked, as if he hardly cared. 'Princess Anne wasn't taken ill, was she?'

'No!' Doug Way came back from his school year diary open on the desk, where he'd been looking at filming possibilities. 'No, that's—'

'Can we freeze frame that?'

'Sure.'

Doug Way froze it. Ben could hardly believe his luck. There were the other two, caught from the front before they really hooded up. A woman in an anorak and a man pulling down his baseball cap. Both black, both mid thirties. When he saw what Ben was looking at, Doug Way coughed.

'That's Frances Scott, isn't it?' Ben asked.

'Which one? No. Some girl who was took ill. Taken ill. Someone in the play, didn't spot which one. Grace Someone?

167

Yeah, these two took her out.'

'And do you know who they are?'

'Never seen them before,' Doug Way lied. 'I understand …from the other kids…she might be the girl's sister, over from somewhere.'

'Abroad.'

'Yeah, some place like that.'

'So they applied for tickets in the normal way?'

The caretaker shrugged.

'Doesn't matter, they're not what I'm interested in.' Ben ran the tape on, but there was nothing more of the three of them: and shortly afterwards, out came HRH and all the rest, as before. 'Can you keep this tape for me?' Ben asked.

'Definitely, no trouble.' Doug Way switched off the machine. 'And you'll be in touch? About the filming?'

'I surely will.'

Doug Way pressed his card like a secret token into Ben's hand.

DOUGLAS WAY

SENIOR PREMISES MANAGER

KENSINGTON GIRLS' HIGH SCHOOL

'Cheers, Doug.'

'Cheers, Ben.'

'Don't worry if you don't hear for a day or two, these things take a while to set up, going through the contracts department.'

'Oh, I know, I know. Don't they?'

And Ben went, using his eyes as little as possible: because into his mind were printed the faces of those two people, one on either side of the girl who Ben was now convinced had to be Frances Scott. He rushed back to Zephon as quickly as he could and found Sandra Alan, the graphic artist they often used in court and anywhere else that cameras were banned. He took her into a sound cubicle to be private, described the faces he'd seen – eyes shut to see, eyes open to correct – and together they made the best job they could of a Photo-fit portrait of two suspected kidnappers.

CONFIDENTIAL FILE

ZEPHON TELEVISION

Telephone Log

BEN MADDOX – PHONE

23rd October

15.00 To Patrick Maddox mobile (0780 3455 3356)
Telephoned brother Patrick, told him I'd got possible evidence of a serious crime. Gave no more details on an insecure line, but Patrick knows who I'm talking about, altho' that's all. He informed me that a diplomat local to the girl's school has complained to the Kensington nick that a white Transit van reg. X01FKM was parked in the residents-only parking zone outside his house prior to the HRH visit to the school, Tuesday 15th, driven off during the evening.
DVLS records show that this is a false number plate. Could be linked?

15.10 Calls to 35 Metropolitan Police switch centres (1212 numbers) and City of London police (020 7601 2222) requesting info. on present whereabouts of the white van.
No joy. They'll 'keep an eye open'. Some of them.

Ben Maddox

From: "Jonny Aaranovitch" jonaar@yahoo.com
To: "Ben Maddox" b.maddox@a.net
Sent: 18.26 23/10
Subject: Re: Robert Freed filming

hi ben

it's the magayana boys here all right (and girl). in the local hotel met some of the drilling crew, just dropped in to one of them how it gets into your lungs, the sugar being burned off. after a sugar story assignment i'd coughed for a fortnight I told him. so did he, he says! didn't push it any further, but he's been out there... bloom might get more!

jonny

CONFIDENTIAL FILE

ZEPHON TELEVISION

Transcript of voice mail

BLOOM RAMSARAN TO BEN MADDOX

23rd October

Ben, it's Bloom. You got Jonny's e-mail? Well, Handsome, how's this? There's a girl in the Freed drilling team, Freed being an equal opportunities company, would you believe, except she's more equal than most because she's got a brilliant mind and she's a one-off. They took her on for her geology degree, name's Irene Porter, and she's well at home on a drilling derrick. I leave you to guess why the men round the rigs leave her alone and she took a shine to me.

I was using my laptop in the hotel bar, she came over, and we started talking computers. 'Hi-ya – oh, you've got a Compaq!' – that sort of thing. 'Get you a drink?' And she tells me how out of date my computer's going to be next year. I'm going, 'Uh?' and she clams up. Well, we're introduced and we're having a drink already, so I change the subject. But at the back end of it, before I say a firm goodbye, I'm off to ring my boyfriend, she lets out this word. Stenocryst. I guess it's s-t-e-n-o-c-r-y-s-t. Leave you to look it up, but I bet you your mortgage that that's your Magayana connection.

Coming back now. See ya!

Ben knocked papers sideways in his swivel-chair race along the desk space to his computer. He cursed at the time it took to get on-line, broadband or not, and at last he found what he was after, on a web site devoted to geology academics.

COLERIN GEOLOGICAL REVIEW

STENOCRYST

A recently discovered mineral crystal of the quartz group. Unlike the quartz found in commercial quantities in Brazil and other parts of the world, stenocryst – as its name implies – is a narrow or compacted form of the mineral. It has a hardness of 7 and a specific gravity of 3.79 (normal commercial quartz has a s.g. of 2.65). It exhibits the same piezoelectric effect (electric voltage when subjected to pressure) but at a much increased rate. Natural high-grade quartz crystal would be superceded by stenocryst, if obtainable in commercial quantities, apart from its use in timekeeping, etc., which would remain unchanged.

Used as a crystal oscillator, providing a clock signal to co-ordinate all activities of the microprocessor, current clock speeds would be increased ten-fold by stenocryst.

NB For some years attempts have been made to manufacture such a quartz variant synthetically but without success. Its main attribute is the ten-fold speed (see above) with which it vibrates in piezoelectric use, thus speeding all computing processes and facilitating a new generation of ultra-fast computers. Its discovery in potentially high quantities would revolutionise the electronics industry throughout the world.

Ben printed it up as fast as he could and set a whirlwind in the newsroom as he raced for Kath Lewis's door.

'Right!' said Kath Lewis. 'What have you got? Where are we?'

'On Magayana?' Ben asked, slowing, holding on to this moment for its professional pleasure.

'On what else? Have I sent you to the Chelsea Flower Show?'

'That's summer, love!'

Kath Lewis looked up at him; but she could stay seated and give a disdainful look as if she were towering above him. 'On Magayana! Your sole assignment so far – that has produced precious little in the way of stuff I can use.'

Ben sat, unasked, smoothed his printouts and flipped his notebook from his pocket, somehow stayed unsmug. 'Summary. Wait till you hear this!'

'I am waiting!'

'First off, I strongly suspect Magayana's sitting on a rare new mineral called stenocryst, it's in the north, under the sugar plantations – and when they dig it out, my theory is that in partnership with us, Magayana stands to be a world leader in electronics. Which will be big stuff, a big deal, the new Industrial Revolution led by John Bull and a rogue state...'

'Cut the Sky News language! Go on...'

Ben *was* going on, talking over her. 'But the fly in the ointment is, Claude Chaumet's in the way. Because there's a danger he could persuade the UN to hold all that up, which would give the USA and others the time to explore for their own stenocryst...'

Kath's eye had long lost its place on the TV beyond Ben. 'And you have this on the evidence of – what?' She held out

175

her hand to take his papers, and shushed him into silence as she read what he'd got. Finally, she looked up, expressionless.

'Chaumet put me on to it,' Ben said, filling the gap left by there being no praise from Kath Lewis. 'The man himself. Talk of unmarked drilling equipment. I've been down his chimney, like you suggested. I did a bit of digging, and Bloom and Jonny have come up with what you've got in your hand...'

'And this is genuine, is it? This isn't Chaumet stringing you along for his own ends? His own tribal ends?' Kath Lewis was fiddling with some other papers on her desk, some documents that were invading her slapping space.

Ben frowned at her; neither she nor the late Len Wyatt had ever suggested that Chaumet wasn't genuine. Was Bill Finch getting at her? Was there a hidden agenda here to do with who had the top line story running at Zephon?

So Ben tested her. 'I think we should go with what we've got,' he said. 'In the ten o'clock. Bring this into the open. *Make* the news.'

'And blow the PM out of the water?' Kath Lewis shook her head. 'Sadly, I've got news for you, Ben Maddox. My bulletin to you. Right now.' She looked up at the big, sweeping hand clock on her wall as she held up one of the intrusive papers. 'The Defence Press and Broadcasting Committee have asked us to sign up to a blackout on Chaumet and Magayana until after the appeal period.'

'What?'

'They've asked us not to report on it.'

Ben slapped his notebook shut. 'I know what a blackout agreement is. I meant "What?" as in *"What!?"*'

'Well, that's what they've done. For the Home Office.

I've had to sign. We always do.'

Ben stared at her. 'That's Dennis Scott,' he said. 'Again.'

'The same.' Kath Lewis shrugged. 'So, what do you make of that, Ben Maddox, before I send you to do a piece on the Eden Project?'

Ben leant his elbows on her desk and clenched his hands in a praying position against his chin. He went on holding her gaze for a few seconds while his brain raced for a decision on whether or not to come out with the bizarre theory he was working on that was closer to home. He'd wanted more to show her before he presented her with it. Could he bear to be laughed out of the office?

He just could. He took the chance.

'There's something going on,' he told her, as she reached down into a deep drawer and poured herself her first red wine of the day. 'It's Dennis Scott who wants silence, isn't it? It's Scott who wants a news blackout. And when else do we get news blackouts?'

'Blacks-out,' Kath Lewis corrected. 'When it's a matter of national security...'

'And...?' Ben prompted, a bit like drawing Meera out when he wanted to show off.

'When there's a hostage situation.'

'Exactly.'

'But when that happens editors and executives are called in, told about it, trusted... They keep us on side.'

'Always?' And he answered his own question, aware of how dangerously cocky he must be sounding. 'We can't say they always do that because we won't always know. It's like you always reckon you can spot a man with a wig; but the men with brilliant wigs aren't in your statistics. It's not the undetected crime—'

'It's the unsuspected!' Kath Lewis finished for him. 'Come on, wonder boy, what are you getting at?'

He told her, top line journalism, a few succinct words. 'Frances Scott, the daughter, has gone missing. She missed her school play, she's not at home, she's said to be unwell when according to her friend she's on top form performing for Princess Anne the night before. She's on video wearing distinctive black nail varnish twice: once on Jonny's camera coming out of the house on the first day of the play; and again that night on CCTV being half carried up Lippard Street away from the school...'

'How do you know it's her?'

'I don't. It's my hunch.'

'Ah!' Another sip. 'So, *assuming* it's her, what's your theory?'

'That the Magayanans have got her. Chaumet's supporters. One of their poets writes about direct action to save the sugar plantations and their tribal lands. Scott is being blackmailed to let Chaumet stay, I know he is, he's going round looking like a man with bad toothache.'

Sip. Sip. Sip. 'Have you got a shred of proof for this?'

'CCTV footage from the school, but it's not conclusive.'

Kath Lewis leaned back in her chair. 'And the boy? There's a son, isn't there?'

'He's not at school, either. Legwork.' Although he didn't mention it was Bloom Ramsaran's also.

'Then for now it's more legwork, and fishing,' Kath Lewis said, eventually. 'Latch on to anything your policeman source can find out – without a word as to why – and get close again to Dennis Scott. Ask him something pointed, but keep it clever.' She looked at a schedule on her computer. 'There's a Home Office briefing on prison reform later today. Go to that instead of Maggie Turton – she won't mind, they're not announcing anything dramatic. You've got time. Read his face, read his mind...'

'OK.' Ben got up.

'And keep it low level. I don't want your ugly mug on the six o'clock.'

'Yes, ma'am.'

'Well, go on, then.' Gulp. And pour.

But by the time Ben had closed Kath Lewis's door behind him, she was reading the blackout request again, and picking up her phone.

Paul Simpson

From:	"Paul Simpson" paul.simpson1@virgin.net
To:	Meera Sharma (E-mail) meerash@allmanpub.co.uk
Sent:	23 October 09:13
Attach:	
Subject:	Geology dinner

Hi Meera,

Just to let you know that tonight's fine for dinner. Looking forward to meeting your partner and briefing him (altho' there's not much to brief) on the geology of northern South America. Very intriguing!

Eight o'clock OK? Don't reply if it is. I've got the address.

Paul

CONFIDENTIAL FILE

ZEPHON TELEVISION

Memo – Ben Maddox to Kath Lewis

SUBJECT: Meetings with Dennis Scott,
23rd October Portcullis House, Westminster

<u>PRISON REFORM</u>

Kath – as predicted, nothing much was announced at this
press conference – beyond the setting up of a government
inquiry into prison food. It's hard to understand why the
Secretary of State for Home Affairs was there himself – 'tho'
I have a theory. I think the meeting might originally have
been called to underline the strength of the government's
case against Claude Chaumet, under a supplementary
question. The guy from the Chronicle tried to ask about
procedures for house arrest of foreign nationals, definitely a
plant. He actually got Chaumet's name out, but he was
dead surprised to be shut up by Scott! The Home Sec. said
he wasn't going into that – but the guy got a wink and a
wave from the Cabinet Office figure present, a sort of, *leave
it, I'll tell you later* message.

I asked this Chronicle guy afterwards – Andy Smith,
little toady with big hair, gets on the late night BBC TV
debates – and he said what a cracking case the government's
got against Chaumet, when it comes out. I'm probably
hopelessly wrong, but I think they're stalling on the
deportation. So why? We know, don't we?

Scott announced the prison food inquiry – boils down to, should the Prison Service or the Health Service foot the bill for prisoners on gluten free and nut allergy diets? Big deal! Not what you'd call a top ministerial matter. Scott seemed set to leave, twelve minutes from coming in through the door to getting up again, looked even worse than before, like a man who hasn't slept in 72 hours, all that public figure bounce gone out of him. So I sounded him out. Well, Bill Finch wasn't there to get upset!

I asked Scott if the number of prisoners on special diets was greater in men's or women's prisons. He didn't know, no one there knew, only guesses – so he said he'd find out and let me know. Remembered me, didn't ask where to send the answer. But I kept on. I asked him if the recent play about Holloway Prison had opened his eyes at all to conditions there. He looked at his people, much shaking of heads, faces saying, 'What play?' he looked at me ready to put me down the way he put me down in the World View interview, so I told him: <u>The one at your daughter's school last week. Wasn't she in it, didn't you see it? Or was she out of the cast before you got to see it?</u> He stared at me, knocked his water glass over, but he'd drained most of it already, fidget drinking. The Cabinet Office matey jumped in and told me my question was an intrusion into privacy – and wrapped the conference up. But outside, while I was talking to Smith from the Chronicle, Scott came over, put an arm out to take hold of one of us. Obviously, Smith thought it was going to be him, but it was me. 'A word, Ben,' he says. <u>Ben!</u>

PRIVATE MEETING

Scott took me into a side room, told his people and his protection officer to wait outside. He looked terrible up close, he's lost the knack of having a decent shave, and his breath was stale, a real 'morning after' mouth. He asked me what I knew about the play at his daughter's school. I said we'd been in touch with the drama department over the possibility of filming there, following up on the Princess Anne/James Bond story in the Evening Standard. I said that the head of drama there had confirmed that his daughter was in the play, and that she'd been taken ill at the end of the first night. I played it all innocent, but Scott knew that I was following up on something. Did I know what his daughter looked like? he asked me. I told him I'd seen her on the morning I'd door-stepped him about Chaumet (he shut his eyes at the name), getting a lift to school wearing her black nails, presumably for the play. He nodded at that. Then I told him I'd seen black nails again later, on CCTV, when someone looking like her was helped home from the school, shortly before Princess Anne and the audience came out. And this time he didn't nod, he just stared at me. He didn't know what to say, except he finished up asking for my mobile number. He said it was handy to have key journalist contacts. *Key journalist!* Kath.

But there's something going on. That man is doing three crucial things at once – having a stab at his job, hiding something, and clutching at straws. So sayeth the prophet. Now to prove it... I'll call in or file later.

Ben

CONFIDENTIAL FILE

Fran Scott – her story 11
(transcribed from tape)

Listen – he's getting edgy, and I'm getting scared all over again; it's like things are coming to a climax. I've never not been scared, but real terror comes and goes, and it's coming now. The woman's out a lot, I can hear that shutter rolling up and back when she goes off, and I know it's working week time, I've been making scratches on the wall like the Count of Monte Cristo. Up to now it's six, but I didn't start straight off. Well, what else to do? Some of the women in Holloway do exercises, keep fit because they want to come out like models; but at least they know they're coming out! I bet they don't give a damn about their figures on Death Row, America, no more than I do...

Although I do keep the brainbox going; who knows, a bit of quick thinking might save me, sometime. I do a few chemistry formulae in my head, and I say the lines of the play over and over to keep from seizing up: get into one of the speeches.

> ***They go on about why am I in here.*** *Good cockney accent!*
> ***On and on! Every visiting, she's nagging away at it,***
> ***my mum. "Why? Why did you have to kill him?"***
> ***Well, she might be used to it, being under the heel,***
> ***taking it, she's been knocked about by two of them,***
> ***first her husband, then my dad. But I wasn't having it,***
> ***I owed it to myself and the kids to get free, didn't I?***
> ***That's the reason I did what I did – I wasn't living a life***
> ***under no one's thumb. And when this stretch is done,***

I won't be anyone's dog! Manslaughter! Huh! It was bloody murder! But I'll be out in four and then I'll be free. (pause)

Yeah, put that in your notebook, Chaplain.

(A long silence) I wish you could put your life back to a previous date, like I can on my computer. I'd go back to that night being in that play – and you can bet I'd keep my eyes wide open backstage!

Anyhow, the good, no, the reasonable news is, before the woman goes off each day, I'm getting to go to the proper lavatory and the shower, and then again at night, so I can work my body functions round that. I'm wearing the grey knickers, I've washed out my others, and she's thrown a white T-shirt into the room, sizes too big, but at least it's clean. Socks are a problem, getting smelly, so I've washed them and left them on the radiator.

And the bathroom cabinet's empty of pills and the razor now. So perhaps they've changed their minds and think I might top myself. Who knows?

When I'm in the washroom I can hear vehicles, some of them heavy like lorries, and men's shouts sometimes, as if they're guiding transport into parking bays or whatever – but it's all far away, and I'm not risking shouting till I can hear people nearer. Who wants that rag round the mouth again? And you can bet it'd be just when I shout 'Help!' that some great big aeroplane comes over low. They're coming over all the time.

I can always count the minutes to him coming in. From the shutter going down to him coming to take out the dirty plate, it's always under five minutes. He can't wait. I get up off the mattress – most of the time I'm lying there huddled,

185

sleeping saves you marking the long, long stretches of being shut up on your own; but he times his visits for after that shutter goes – and I make sure I'm over by the table by then. And I still can't figure it out if he's weighing me up like the hangman looking at a prisoner for the drop. Or is he excusing himself for what he's doing? I think that could be it. Because he's definitely edgy.

I ask him. Today, I ask him. In he comes, round the door, baseball hat pulled low, neckerchief round his face, locks the door behind him, leaning on the wall the way he always does, no move to clear the plate, just looking at me. All I ever see is his eyes.

I ask him. 'What is it with my dad? What is it you want?'

He doesn't say anything, just goes on looking at me, making up his mind about something. And as he pushes up off the wall I hope like hell it's not what he's got to do to me that's making him edgy. But he comes over to me – I'm at the table – and he opens his hands like a Pontius Pilate. 'We have to do what's right for our people,' he says. And there's a shine to those eyes like a suicide bomber or a terrorist fanatic: you can never find the words to change the mind of a man staring like that. I get up and back off as he sits on his favourite perch – the edge of that table.

'Don't worry,' he says. 'Not yet.' And my guts run to water. NOT YET! So, sometime?! He sees the look on my face. 'Could be, not ever, girl. It's a decision not down to me.' I get the washed hands again.

It is political, I know, it's not money – because our family hasn't got money, not the sort these people would want from a kidnap: they'd have gone for Ali Rakad's daughter, Noor, he owns half of Knightsbridge; someone like that, we've got a few in our school. I've been thinking all this out. So if it's Dad, what's he in charge of? Prisons? If it had been some prisoner they want let out of jail, would this man and woman here be foreign, talking about 'their people'? No, they're political activists – and they want something my dad can give them that isn't money, and isn't about prisons.

So, what? I've spent a week lying on that mattress going over all this. See, he's Home Office, my father, not Foreign Office – and they're foreign. So is it immigration? Is it deportation? My dad's shouted most at about deportation. And this man's given me clues, trying to excuse himself for doing what he's got to do, he's talked about a country or somewhere with two sets of people living in it, and him and his mother being in prison after his father was killed, so it's got to be some divided country, one lot in power, the other under the heel. But, where? God, why couldn't I have taken more interest in Current Affairs? Eh, Gussie? Why did we have to make each other laugh instead of paying attention?

So I take a chance. I want to get into this man's head, because being on his side might be the one chance I ever get to be let out, when the woman's not here.

'What happens to people in your country when they get sent back?' I ask him. I put on the sort of face that looks as if I might know stuff. 'Important people, political?'

He shuts his eyes, a long blink. Again, he's thinking, perching there, what to say, what not to say. And he suddenly flicks his fingers, like someone used to worry beads who hasn't got any, and he puts a hand to his throat and draws it across. Death!

'That's terrible!'

'It's terrible for him, it's terrible for our people...' His eyes have suddenly filled up with tears; all at once he's like a

father, someone picturing his little kids back home being massacred or starved.

'And you think my father can stop this happening?'

He takes a year to slowly nod. And because he's gone too far, and he knows he's gone too far – definitely if I tell the woman what I know now – he gets up and unlocks himself out of the room, fast. Leaves the dirty plate.

And all at once I have a stupid ray of hope shining in through these no-window rooms. Because this means my father can save me. If he plays ball with them, if he doesn't do whatever it is these people want him not to do, I can get out of this place alive. And my dad would always put me before everything else, wouldn't he, even being who he is?

Wouldn't he?

If they make me do a recording on this recorder again, I'll tell my dad, I'll let him know I'm on these people's side, to do what they say... (tape clicks on pause, then restarts) ...but for now I'll take the chewing gum off the hole in the cassette and play the other side, old Aretha. Loud. She can cheer me up. 'Say a little prayer for you'! No. Make it for me, eh?

(tape clicks off)

PICCADILLY LINE UNDERGROUND

'Hurt her. Make her scream. Send some agony through that phone line. Make her father vomit at the sound of it.'

D gave his instructions to Laurina Modeste as if he were quietly discussing the news in the *Herald Tribune* that he was holding up in front of him. But unlike the last time, today he wasn't speaking in code. She had boarded the underground train at Heathrow Terminal Four, heading towards the station that serves Terminals One, Two and Three; and the New York newspaper had been her signal to get into this particular carriage. The Heathrow loop of track under the airport is the longest stretch between stations on the Piccadilly Line, ideal for a talk with passengers who have either just boarded humping heavy luggage, or preparing to alight for their arrivals or departures at one of the other terminals – no one has any attention to spare for a quiet couple sitting behind a newspaper.

'Are we gettin' to that?' Laurina asked, as if he'd just now requested her to post a letter, not torture a girl.

'The mother and the boy's not in London, I did tell you that...?' D checked.

Laurina kept her eyes on the unsettled passengers. 'It was me told you he wasn't in school.'

'Could be Scotland. There's relatives there. I've got a few addresses, and I'm going to get to him soon. But things are quiet temporarily, too quiet.' D thumped the armrest, but gently. 'Our man needs a push, a good scary push to remind him we mean business. He's had the appeal and plenty of time to study it, he doesn't have to wait the full term to give his decision.'

'OK.'

'Is your man up to doing it?'

'He's not my man, no way! But I'll see he won't let us down.'

Laurina wriggled in her seat as the tube train began to slow. People shuffled in the carriage and luggage swayed. 'Yeah, I'll see to that!'

'See if that works. Meantime, you've had no sniff of anyone around, no Special Branch or police, no one suspicious?'

'No one.' Laurina Modeste looked the other way, didn't tell him about the drugged-up kid and the dog.

'Because if this has got out, this PM would always take the state hard line – never give in to violent pressure. But the girl's father, he's different… And he knows how long he's got.'

'An' he has the say?'

'It's on his desk, his responsibility, that's how this sort of government works.' He stared ahead across the carriage, dropped his voice into his throat, a 'bottom line' sound. 'I'm counting the days, then you kill the girl, OK? We'll soon have the boy. The man's got to know we're serious. Zero tolerance, it works both ways.'

'Jesus forgive me, we're serious all right!'

'Good. And here's what you came for – expenses.' D passed her a Switch card. 'The usual PIN.' Laurina took the card and put it into her Oyster wallet. 'Everything else OK?' He was at his newspaper again.

'Course it is.'

'Then read this, you'll see why we've got to push this on fast.' He passed her a folded sheet of paper from behind the financial page. 'And be sure – I want a good, painful screaming and hollering through that phone!' he said. 'I'll inform you how we'll meet for the pick-up of the tape. And make it real nasty, don't you hold back!'

'Man, I never hold back!' Laurina said, as she stood to get out, leaving D on the train to travel the route back towards the capital. 'Don't you worry – I'm in this for real.'

LEYTON E10

Meera Sharma was sitting on the overlarge sofa of the rented flat like a woman pleased to have her own separate surname. The moment Ben came through the door he could see there was trouble, she was reading the *Evening Standard* magazine – and she never read the *Standard* beyond page two of the news.

It was late, and he'd been to brother Pat's place out at Biggin Hill to give him copies of his rogues' gallery of Photofit pictures.

Meera stood up and just stared at him. She was clearly close to tears. For a split second Ben thought she might be going to come at him; but she just went on staring, and finally hissed, 'Maddox, we've got a phone here. I've got a mobile phone. You've got a mobile phone. OK, so you've been working, but could you let me know? No! *Where the hell have you been?*'

Ben took off his reefer coat and threw it on an armchair. This was serious! Meera had never come on like this before. Had she been worried about him? Or did she think he might have been with some other woman – Sandra Alan, the graphic artist, or Kath Lewis? Or Bloom Ramsaran? At whom he suddenly felt an unwelcome roll in his stomach.

'For God's sake what's up, Meer? I'm on an assignment, I got involved, time went, I headed home, I didn't think you'd take on like this! 'Strewth, you work nine to five, a journalist works five to nine: five am to nine pm…'

'And beyond!'

'Yeah, and beyond. And I'm sorry if I spoilt the meal, and your evening. I'm really sorry.' Ben went over to touch her, to try to kiss her, but the *Evening Standard* became the barrier, rolled into a club.

'Don't! Please! Not now. You let me down!'

'OK, well… I'll go hungry, but do you want to know what I've found out?' Because that's what it was about, he'd been following leads and getting somewhere. Perhaps.

But what did she mean, he'd let her down?

'I don't want to know *anything* about what you found out. Ever!' Meera walked towards the door that led to the corridor, and the bedroom. 'Maddox, do you know who was here tonight? Do you remember who you asked me to invite, if he'd come – and I told you might be here tonight, to phone me and check?'

And that churn in Ben's stomach doubled, deepened into guilt. Oh, no! How could he have forgotten? Half-good journalists don't forget that sort of thing, even though they've been excited in a revelation, wrapped up in a search. Headwork, that's what he should have done as well as legwork. And, of course, it seemed impossible to have forgotten now that she'd reminded him. Talking about Magayana and its minerals, Meera had offered up one of their young writers on the publisher's educational list – Paul Simpson, who had got a book published with them on the geography and geology of South America. He could come for a Marks and Spencer pie and pudding supper, she suggested, and Ben had jumped at the chance to know what was under its neighbours in the rest of Magayana's corner of South America.

And there, out of the corner of his eye, on the hatch through to the kitchen, Ben saw a bottle of white wine that Paul must have brought. Like Kath Lewis, Ben and Meera were red wine people. So there it was, warming in the heat of the anger in the room. Oh, God! What a bummer! What a terrible thing to do! To forget a possible date, let a bloke down, and not even to phone. To blow someone out like that, a man prepared to give up his evening to help him. What a shit Ben Maddox was!

He threw himself into the armchair, on top of his reefer. 'Oh, Jesus, Meer! Oh, God! Oh!'

'Why don't you throw in Allah and Mohammed, you turd?!' Ben put his face in his hands. When there was nothing to be said, there really was nothing to be said.

'His phone number's over there. Next to the book he left, open at the page you want.' She wouldn't unfold her arms to point at it.

'I'm sorry! I'll phone him, OK?'

Meera swung the door open almost smack against the wall to get out to the bedroom. With no doubt in either head as to where Ben would spend the night.

He shouted another apology and went over to the open book.

The geology of this part of South America is uncomplicated.

Like parts of its neighbours – Suriname, Guyana, and Venezuala – Magayana sits on metamorphic, plutonic and volcanic rocks. Quartz occurs in veins, occurring in the late phase of magma-mineral precipitation, one of the last to form because of the lower temperature at which it becomes solid. These quartz strata and their variants continue relatively unchanged through to the Pacific Ocean.

Attached to the page by a paper clip was a handwritten note.

Your stenocryst would be compressed into a narrow strata through 'folding' – therefore altho' it's highly likely to be present in the continuing strata it might take some finding. P

Ben read through the marked section and the note several times. He telephoned Paul Simpson but only got the answerphone into which he made an elegant apology – the more elegant because he realised the full importance of Paul Simpson's writings. Whatever was under Magayana by way of stenocryst was under those other South American countries too. So the president of Magayana – and the British – were in a race against time: to extract and market their revolutionary electronics 'gold' before neighbouring countries and their international partners found it as well and got in on the act.

He went to the bathroom; the bedroom door was firmly shut; and came back to make himself comfortable on the sofa with his reefer coat for a blanket. And his sleeping thoughts, disgracefully, were not of Meera on the other side of that wall, but of Claude Chaumet and what he was trying to do – stay in Britain, keep up his offensive on the United Nations, halt the rape of his people's land and fight for their rights to a share in their nation's natural wealth.

And, of course, the sugar people could have been cut in: but this was tribal and racist, too, wasn't it?

WESTMINSTER SW1

When the PM wants to see you, you go: even Ministers of State have to drop everything to obey the call. From his flat in Victoria, Dennis Scott chose to get a breath of air and walk to the PM's office in the Palace of Westminster, talking to his 'prot' officer who had come with the car.

Or, not talking. The 'prot' officer on shift did the

nondescript talking while Dennis Scott walked, well inside himself, recognised by nobody with a face so haggard and different from the one often seen on television. Scott had been told by the Cabinet Office the sole item on the PM's agenda – Claude Chaumet – and he knew the only question he would be asked would be why hadn't the foreign politician's appeal against deportation been refused yet? His appeal was in, a decision could be announced. Why wasn't the man on a plane back to Magayana?

Scott had stayed at the Victoria flat to avoid all the domestic stuff at Kensington Mews, his mobile phone on the charger and switched on all the time. But he had heard nothing – and when he met the PM, he was as low as he'd ever been in his life.

Who was brisk.

'Come in, Dennis.' No 'coffee?' or 'a little snifter?' Not today.

And serious indeed, because no one else was allowed to stay in the room: Scott wasn't even invited to sit.

The PM looked as bad as Scott did. Where were the youthful, carefree, bright eyes of student life and Opposition days when plans for a better world were being made over pints of real ale? Where had their pomp gone, these two?

'Chaumet. He's got to go!' the PM growled.

'Well, that was the drift of the last meeting, I know, Prime Minister—' Scott couldn't even call him 'Alan' the way Fran and Caitlin could. 'But—'

'Then do it, Dennis. You've made your decision, you don't have to wait until the final date for his appeal. It's in, and you're disallowing it.'

'It's not that straightforward. I said I'd wait until the fourteen days were up.'

'It's perfectly straightforward. We want him out – out he goes!' The PM with his dandruff, a cold sore, and yak's eyes hardly looked like a man this Thursday morning who was in the middle of a passionate love affair. And he had the snap of a thrashing croc. 'There's no need to wait. Get it done!' He lowered his voice, although the room was regularly swept for bugs. 'We've isolated him, we've intercepted his mail, we've cut off his phone, blacked-out his internet and severed his e-mail; he hasn't got a server any more. But, OK, that works for a few days while no one knows. There's press sniffing round, though. You had one of them on TV, I had him at my briefing...'

'Maddox. Ben Maddox. Zephon.'

'So do it fast! He's been in to Chaumet, got in the house – God bless our security – we've got an MI5 picture of him leaving through the front door at Blackheath. And the intelligence spooks have run the transmission tapes again, he's been out there to Magayana, they were shown with your interview – and now I've had President Gomez on the phone. Maddox is sniffing! He's on to more than he should be...'

'But you've asked for a news blackout on Chaumet...'

'Which as you well know is voluntary.'

'You've got hooks...'

'Never mind the hooks! You've got a pen! Sign the bloody deportation!' The PM sneezed, a persistent cold these days.

Dennis Scott picked up his briefcase. 'I'll go over the papers again...'

Sneeze again, and wipe. 'Go over them with your pen! Write your damned name all over them! And sign "disallowed" at the bottom! I can't for the life of me understand why you're dithering! You know how much hangs on this deal!'

Scott turned towards the door, turned back again. He barely got the words out for his lack of voice: 'Yes. And a lot more than you think!' he just about managed. 'Alan.' And he went.

ZEPHON TELEVISION

South Bank Studios – London SE1

INTERNAL MEMO

SIR REGINALD FEWSTER TO KATH LEWIS, PRODUCER WORLD VIEW

I understand that Ben Maddox has had an interview with Claude Chaumet. I should very much like to see his notes on the meeting.

RF

Thursday 26th October

SOUTH BANK SE1

Ben was in no mood for a roasting. Already he'd been roasted by Meera – fit for Coffee Express. Now, sitting in the newsroom, no joy had come through from brother Pat on the Photo-fit pictures, and the phone was deathly quiet on the stolen number-plate hunt. One day you're up, floating on air, the next you're down, because the feather of success needs continual puffing up to keep it in the air. Yesterday was always yesterday; today is today. With a summons to see Kath Lewis.

But Ben went in looking bouncy, value for money, the man for the job, switched the confidence on as he pushed at the door; it was just a shame that he'd left his button-down shirt collar unbuttoned-down.

'Hi, Kath! Progress report?'

'Nope. You'd have been through that door to see me an

hour ago if you'd got anything worth reporting.'

'I wouldn't say that...' Ben sat down.

'Don't crease your trousers, it's a quickie.'

'Yes?' Ben got up.

'Your notes on the Chaumet interview. Your "down-the-chimney" job.'

Ben nodded. He'd typed everything up and filed it like a good little cub reporter.

'I want them.'

'Sure. A script? Are we doing a piece after all? Has Dennis Scott pronounced?' There'd been nothing on the wires about a Home Secretary deportation decision, but this sounded as if the news blackout might have been lifted. Well, Ben was always up for an appearance on the channel – who wouldn't be?

'Sir Reginald wants to read your notes. Just get them for me, will you?'

'Sure. But, Sir Reg, why would he want them? He's not hands-on, is he?' Ben was truly puzzled, and starting to get cross, which wasn't difficult this morning. If his memory of the conversation and his noted conclusions of the Chaumet visit were under scrutiny at Board Room level, that could only mean one thing – his journalism was under discussion. Was there a suspicion that he was 'dodgy' on his facts? Did they think Ben Maddox had to be watched?

'Sit down again.'

'Why?' People ask you to sit to save you falling over at bad news. She'd just told him it was a quickie. Had he gone too far, over the back gardens of Blackheath? Had there been a complaint? Or was the government getting at Sir Reg? Either way, a junior reporter could be sacrificed quicker than you splat a mozzie.

'Just bloody sit!' Kath used the slapping space on her desk for its proper purpose. 'And listen.'

Ben sat.

'Who owns this company?' Kath Lewis asked, but her voice had dropped; Ben had never heard her speaking in such a low register, not even in the control suite during transmission.

'Zephon plc.'

'Right, and who owns Zephon plc?'

And before Ben gave Kath the answer that he well knew, its implication had hit him: its implication in all its simplicity. Of course! Of course! 'Zephon Inc., New York, a division of Zephon International,' he recited.

'Right.'

'Now tell me who comes off second best in the electronics field if the UK is ahead in the market with Magayana's stenocryst?'

Ben hardly bothered saying, 'The Americans.' It was so obvious now. The Zephon America people probably had fingers, hands, and buckets in American computer shares. At present the Americans were the world leaders in the field – no wonder Zephon International wanted Chaumet up and fighting his corner to stop Britain taking the lead.

'I get it!' Ben exploded. 'Len Wyatt was a tool, and I'm a tool...' He suddenly pushed back the chair with such force that it fell over, his head light with the sudden drain of blood from the brain in his rising anger. *Bringing him on! Go doorstep the Home Secretary: interview him live on air! Stay exclusive to the Chaumet story! Get involved, get to care, have to sleep on the sofa!* Ben couldn't wait to get out of the building, to go and tell anyone who would listen what cruds Zephon were. 'How do you want my resignation?' he shouted at Kath Lewis, 'Will this do?' And he ripped out his Zephon press pass and threw it, not onto the desk, but at her. It hit her on the shoulder and fell into her lap. 'Because I came here as a journalist, not a paid lackey!'

'Aren't Zephon right? Don't we want justice for black Maganayans?' Kath Lewis seemed to be trying to stay in control of this, but she had stood, Ben's press pass had fallen to the floor, and she was leaning forward over her desk. 'Does whatever Zephon wants make the cause wrong?'

'Cause? It's not a cause – it's an agenda! And I'm the patsy in the middle.' Ben picked up the fallen chair and made for the door. He was out of this! There were ways to earn a living where you could sleep at night, in your own bed.

'You're not the patsy in the middle, Ben Maddox! Chaumet's people are! And would you listen to this?'

'No, I wouldn't!' He had hold of the door handle.

'Listen to this, you stupid little show-off!' Kath Lewis screeched it, so loudly that her secretary came to the internal door and had to be waved away. 'What if we make it fair by what we're doing? What if no one's an outright winner, not the British, not the Yanks? What if the wealth is shared between other peoples as poorly off as the Magayanans – *as well as* the Magayanans? What if some other South American peoples get their spoils?'

'I don't follow – and I don't want to!' But Ben had dropped his hold on the door handle.

'You've met Chaumet, you've got as good an idea as any what sort of man he is. What if by delaying his deportation the government is persuaded to go hand-in-hand internationally with the Americans on this? Fair shares for all, never mind the PM's problems and party politics? Wouldn't Chaumet want to see under-privileged peoples in Guyana and neighbouring countries benefit as well? Don't you think he might be that sort of person? And if we worked internationally like that, wouldn't the Magayanan president be forced to let Chaumet's people in on the deal?'

Ben paused, and his leg ached, standing there on one foot ready to go, but not going.

'Have you ever cut sugar?' Kath Lewis went on.

Ben shook his head.

'It's hard, dirty, die-young work. Would you rather go on doing that as a Magayanan, or would you rather have your land used for mechanical mining on a mineral that will make so much more money than sugar ever could – and improve your lifestyle beyond comprehension?'

Ben stood square again, facing Kath Lewis. 'The latter, obviously, if it's achievable.'

'So.' Kath Lewis sat down. 'That's where I'm coming from. Forget Zephon or anyone upstairs or over the sea. That's my credo. That's why Kath Lewis and Len Wyatt were chasing this story.'

Ben nodded, slowly.

'And you work directly for me.' She stooped to the floor and picked up his press pass. 'Don't you?'

He took a deep breath. 'Yes,' he said, quietly.

'Then go and get your notes and keep Sir Reg happy. And remember, when you walk out over your conscience you'll be walking out after me!' Saying that, she threw Ben's press pass back at him, which he caught. 'And bring them in here and we'll open a bottle of Merlot. If there's anything red spilt on my carpet, Ben Maddox, it's not going to be blood.'

REPUBLIC OF MAGAYANA

REQUISITION NOTICE

TO THE TOWNSPEOPLE OF GRAND FLEUVE AND PETIT FLEUVE

NOTICE is hereby given that the lands known
as Grand Fleuve Plantation and Petit Fleuve
Plantation are the subject of a compulsory purchase
(Government Requirement Requisition Order 1302)
as decreed in the Parliamentary Upper Chamber of
Magayana on
Wednesday 15th October last.

THOSE with deed entitlements to these
lands should present such deeds at the
State Land Registry in Magellan within twenty-eight
days from the date of this notice
when compensation will be assessed.

COMPENSATION is at the discretion of
the Honourable Minister of Home Affairs based
on the equivalent of 500 Magayanan
Dollars per hectare.

SIGNED AND DATED
Friday 17th October by the
Honourable President Jorge Gomez, MMP.

Still in her coat, Laurina Modeste unfolded the paper that D had given her and spread it on the kitchen table.

'This Gomez pig, he's not wasting time!' she said to Baptiste. 'Pres-i-dent! He'll have our lands for his president breakfast tomorrow!'

'No big surprise to me!' Baptiste was rooting round in the wall cupboard, sliding cans, pushing packets aside. Now he stopped to read the notice, which brought an angry clicking in his throat. 'We should've cut him down like cane all those years ago! We should've united and shown how our people cannot be divided and ruled...'

While Laurina was fixing him hard with a cobra stare. 'An' speaking of doing violence—'

'What?'

'D wants the girl hurt. This Scott man needs a kick in the ass, and a good screamin' and hollerin' tape down the phone is the short cut. He reckons. He's ordering.'

'Yes?' Baptiste turned from the table. For Laurina his face showed no emotion. 'When?'

She shrugged. 'Soon as. When you can work up the guts.'

Baptiste folded his arms at her. 'You do know that girl is not the sacrifice in this – we are!'

'And willing!'

'Certain – and willing! I've seen the insides of worse prisons than I'll get sent to here.'

Laurina laughed, mirthless, like a magpie call. 'If you get that luxury an' not Gomez's rope.'

Baptiste flicked his fingers. 'If Scott gets his daughter back, and the man *is* the Home Secretary, could be he'll see we don't get sent back. Give us asylum maybe. Real asylum, if we treat the girl gentle and his grudge don't grow too great.'

Now it was Laurina who folded her arms. 'Dear Jesus, what is it this man is saying to me under all that?'

'What I'm saying is, that girl can act. We seen her act. If she can act the screamin' and hollerin' on the tape, perhaps we get leniency if things don't pan out right...'

The look on Laurina Modeste's face said everything anyone can say about contempt: real, superior contempt for a snivelling show of cowardice from the man who wasn't up to a challenge when it came. 'You no-good coward!' she spat at him. 'First, we are not intendin' to get caught after this – D's got passports and everything, we're goin' to Brazil till Chaumet wins the next election – and, second, you said you're up for anything, I told D you're the man for the job... Huh!'

'Killing, if it ever came to it! Killing's different from torturing. Killing's clean! I prayed for killing, prayed for it for me when I was in Magellan Jailhouse!'

'All the same, you're going to do it, boy – or I'm going to do it, Jesus help me! Right?' Laurina Modeste's aggressive, determined face was so different this morning from the soft, sexy come-on she'd shown to Doug Way at the start of the campaign. She was a hard, determined terrorist supported in her fight by her Saviour. 'Right? Right? We're going to do it! A good wapping like you give a bad dog – I've had that off my pa, and off the minister, and Scott's had that at his public school you can bet, so he won't reckon that as *real* harm.'

Augustin Baptiste took in a deep breath, held it, and as he let it out he nodded.

'Get fit, then.' Laurina opened a can of Lilt. 'An' what are you rooting round in that cupboard for? A coca can of courage?'

'Nothing. Checking what we've got, that's all.' He shut the cupboard door.

'Because if it's those headache tablets of yours, I've thrown them down the sluice. Saw you'd left 'em in the washroom, reckoned the girl might overdose or something, spoil the plans.'

'Why the hell did you throw them?'

'Because too much of that stuff around is dangerous. I got plenty of them in my bag. You get a headache, you ask me. Fact, I might take a couple of as'prin myself, partnered up with a pain like you!'

To which Augustin Baptiste had nothing to say.

'Now I'm going to go and find you something suitable for what you're going to do.' Said by Laurina Modeste as if she were going out looking for a spanner to tweak a slow engine.

CONFIDENTIAL FILE

Fran Scott – her story 12
(transcribed from tape)

*It's not him, it's the woman who's brought the food in the last
two times. And that roller shutter hasn't been up or down for at
least two of my scratches on the wall. Something's changing, I
can tell that. Also, I had my shower this morning but they
didn't let me have another bathroom visit last night.*

*Then the man does come in, and he's looking really edgy
again. His neckerchief isn't so tight round his face, I can see
the bridge of his nose, and he's blinking a lot. He wants this,
the cassette recorder, so I give it to him. This tape you're
listening to is safe up in the air brick where I'm keeping it, my
chewing gum over the little hole, and I hope like hell that he
doesn't have a list of what music he gave me to listen to – but
all he wants is to change the batteries. Says he's making sure
they don't run out when he needs it – and he lets me keep the
recorder. So what's that all about?*

*And it's while he's changing the batteries – and I'm seeing a
bit of a shake on his hand – that we both hear the roller shutter
going up, and down again. She's gone out – but this time he
doesn't change. Somehow it's as if she's in the room with us.
He's different. I can hear his breath snorting down his nose on
the inside of the scarf.*

*But while the routine's changed, and he's changed, and even
the batteries have changed, I'm still the same. What I've got
doesn't change – dread fear! It doesn't, it can't. The knowing
something's going to happen to you but you don't know what –
that fear doesn't change; you've still got an inside that must be*

pitted to hell with all those shots of scare that hit you every time you think of tomorrow and where you'll be – or what you'll be!

Like before, though, I'm thinking how I can wheedle round him without it being seen the wrong way, how I can get on his side but without any come-on. How I can just get him back to the way he's been before. And I suddenly say what I've been thinking about all night; if it was night; if they haven't completely disoriented me, because the light through the washroom window's so gloomy, it could be any time. Anyway, I've been listening to some of the things he says, like the way he calls any soft drink a 'coca'. And who says that? Brigitte Vernay, from school, in the drama group. And where's she from?

'It's not Africa, is it?' I ask him, out of nowhere. 'Where you're from.' He's just putting the cassette recorder onto the table, hands still shaking, playing a snatch of music to check the thing's working. And what I've said makes him look over at me, just a snap look, the cassette clattering down – today he won't look at me for long. 'Because I know African talk,' I carry on somehow, 'we've got girls at the school. And it's not the Caribbean.' Now he takes his hands away from putting the recorder to rights and hitches up his neckerchief above his nose. 'But we've got someone from Guyana, she was in the play. You're South American, aren't you?' I almost put 'Baptiste' on the end but that would be a really big mistake.

And I know I'm right, I can tell I've scored one. All I see are his eyes but they tell me so much. Like a dog's. So I play my ace card. I say it very casually, because that's how you play an ace when you want a reaction. 'My school raised two thousand pounds for the earthquake victims in Santa de Merida,' I told him. 'We did a concert. And we signed the World's Children's Petition against the dictatorship in San

Cresto, for all those downtrodden people. Both South America...'

He's looking at the cassette, at the floor, anywhere, not saying anything.

'... So you give me your petition for my father, let me take it to him, and see if me being out in the world working for you isn't better than being locked in here like a hostage.' He looks at me strangely: well, I am a hostage, aren't I?

Then he clears his throat, and my heart starts going. The judge's verdict – he's going to say something crucial to me.

'Our cause is just, girl.' His voice is high up in his head, nervous of something. 'Our people are as bad off as San Cresto peasants, worse. And our earthquake isn't any earth tremor, it's a powerful, shaky president and his ruling tribe that's crushing us.' He closes his eyes, seeing something, or recalling it. Then he recites some poetry: lines about forcing the hand across the sea, the hand that understands action instead of words, and, 'Strike at their sons as they strike at you!' he finishes off.

I remember that because my gut goes pow! with the message. 'Strike at you!'

'Daughters as well as sons?' I ask him. And he doesn't answer. But like someone who can't trust himself with you, he pulls back off the table and unlocks himself out through the door.

Yes! Something's going to happen soon – and I've got the worst feeling in the world that it's not going to be long before it does. He's had the message! And if you ever get this tape, his name's Baptiste, and he's with a big woman, and they're South American, and we're near Heathrow, and I'm just about at the end of it... (sobbing)

(tape clicks off – then, silence to the end of the reel –this is the final recorded message)

HOUNSLOW, MIDDLESEX

Augustin Baptiste went back into Fran's cell almost immediately, was within a click of hearing her talking into the recorder. He'd never come back this soon before and he caught her red-faced, quickly switching cassettes. In his hand was the Magayana requisition notice, which he held out between his fingers for her to see.

'I got this explanation to give...' he said.

'Magayana...' Fran read the words. She knew it was somewhere not far from where 'coca' Brigitte Vernay came from.

'You got it – and these are our lands.' Baptiste held the paper steadyish as Fran read it. 'I'm telling you so you know...'

Fran went rigid, her reddened face draining to a whitewash. 'So I know what?' She could hardly bring herself to say it. 'So I know something before I die? The reason why I'm a sacrifice?'

Baptiste folded the paper and tucked it away inside his shirt. 'Just so you know,' he said.

Fran sat at the table, Anne Boleyn in the Tower. Suddenly she felt almost calm – her one thought now to get the cassette that was in her hand into its hiding place so that someone, one day, might know what had happened.

Still just inside the door, Baptiste slowly slid down the wall onto his haunches, looking across and up at Fran. 'You've heard tell of genocide, I know,' he said in a quiet voice. 'You've heard of the Balkan countries in your lifetime, and the tries Adolf Hitler made to wipe out the Jews in past time...'

Fran would have nodded but her neck had tightened.

This was some sort of final clearing of his conscience.

'...Well, that's what Gomez is doing to us. Only it's not open shooting and killing – though he's done his torturing and disappearing of people – but it's economic. He's shrivelled our sugar, he's about to take our lands, and he's leaving us black Magayanans in poverty to die from starvation.'

Fran stayed staring at him, petrified of his next move to stand up, never mind that again the man was crying.

'You ever seen a child die of starvation?' Baptiste stopped, to regain some control over his voice. 'It don't take long – 'tho in the finish it always takes longer than you want. After last year's harvest was left to rot we buried too many old and too many young, and the weeping and the wailing is a sound I carry in my ears louder than any prison screams. And there's no other way we've got to feed ourselves...'

The cassette tape in Fran's hand was becoming slippery with the sweat of holding it beneath the table, but she didn't move a muscle. She still couldn't. So much was coming out that would enable her to identify this man later, she knew now that she was finished. Her only hope would be to get him caught and her ordeal known.

'You've got a brother...' Baptiste was going on; and immediately he held up his hands to Fran as she shouted at him.

'You leave him alone!'

'Don' worry, he's all right. I'm just saying, you've got a brother, Michael...'

Now Fran was feeling nothing inside, it was as if her nerve endings had been frozen.

'And I had a boy, Michel. Yeah.' He stopped again. 'I

had a boy, my Michel...' Now he got up, pinched at his wet eyes with his fingers. 'Just so you know,' he said. 'We got to change your father's mind before the date on this paper...' And without another word he let himself out of the room; but being sure to lock it from the other side – although Fran couldn't have moved just then even if he'd left it wide open. The way hope dies.

CONFIDENTIAL FILE

FAX FAX FAX FAX FAX FAX

To: Ben Maddox,
Zephon Television   020 773 6060

From: West Drayton Police   01895 51213

Re your enquiry false number plates, white
van, homeless victim of mugging statement
includes reference to X1 and KM or FM.
Similarity to X01 FKM?

Please ring WPC Samantha Reynolds on the
number you have if interested.

Sam Reynolds

WPC H751

CONFIDENTIAL FILE

ZEPHON TELEVISION

Transcript of telephone conversation,

Ben Maddox to Claude Chaumet. NUMBER WITHHELD
FRIDAY 25TH OCTOBER:

Ben Maddox:
 Mr Chaumet?

Claude Chaumet:
 Who is this, please?

Ben Maddox:
 Ben Maddox, Zephon Television.

Claude Chaumet:
 Ah, Mr Maddox. You are the second person from the outside world to contact me today...

Ben Maddox:
 Really? Who else, Mr Chaumet?

Claude Chaumet:
 (Pause) Will you believe, Mr Scott...?

Ben Maddox:
 The Home Secretary? Has he made a decision?

Claude Chaumet:

No. He sends a note here, in the hands of the police. I am thinking it's his decision on my appeal, arriving by motor cycle messenger. I open it with shaking fingers.

Ben Maddox:

But it isn't? It's not the decision?

Claude Chaumet:

No, sir. I must wait for that. In the packet is an envelope for returning while the messenger waits outside. And there is a simple question for answering in the envelope.

Ben Maddox:

Yes?

(Long pause)

Claude Chaumet:

This question, it asks, do I know of any plan to involve a third party – at first I do not understand the meaning of the 'third party'...

Ben Maddox:

Just, someone else. Not you and not him.

Claude Chaumet:

Yes, I understand. He is considering my appeal – and have I sanctioned, or do I know of, any violent action in support of my case...? Have I ever issued a deadline of ten days for the resolution of this affair in my favour?

(Long pause)

Ben Maddox:

And do you? Have you?

Claude Chaumet:

I do not! I know there is talk of direct action, you have
seen the poem by one of our people...

Ben Maddox:

Sure.

Claude Chaumet:

But I am not part of any such action. I am a pacifist,
I fight for my people in courts, with United Nations, I
have fear that direct action does me harm, not good.

Ben Maddox:

So Scott thinks someone, or some people, might be hurt?
Violent action, like a kidnapping and an execution – with
a ten day deadline? And he's checking that you're not in
on it?

Claude Chaumet:

I do not know what he thinks. He asks me the question,
this is all. I reply with a big 'No' on his paper, and I lick
the envelope and I seal it with my seal... And I must still
wait for his decision.

Ben Maddox:

Mr Chaumet, this confirms what I suspect, the lead I'm
following. *(Long pause)* You see, someone, I believe, has
taken his daughter...

Claude Chaumet:

Mr Scott's daughter?

Ben Maddox:

...And the wife and son have left the family home, the boy isn't in school. Nor's the girl, they say she's unwell – in the country to recover. But I think otherwise.
(*Silence, longest pause so far*)

Claude Chaumet:

What did you want, telephoning to me?

Ben Maddox:

To be honest, to ask you the same thing. To be assured that you're not in on any kidnap.

Claude Chaumet:

Mr Maddox! I told you before—

Ben Maddox:

I know, and I'm sorry to be asking for your word. But it's all by way of being on your side. Now, the sixty-four million dollar question – do you know what they're drilling for? What they've found under your sugar lands?

Claude Chaumet:

Gold? Silver? Platinum? What does it matter if we have no share in it?

Ben Maddox:

It's stenocryst – a sort of quartz. It's a mineral that will revolutionise computers. It'll do more for Gomez than any gold and silver, and Britain, too, because we're partners. *(Pause)* And it'll change the balance of power in the electronics world, hit America and the Far East for six...

(Long pause)

Claude Chaumet:

Well, well, well. So we can say that things are becoming very clear...

Ben Maddox:

Clearer, anyhow. And given what I've told you, who do you think might be masterminding the kidnap of the Home Secretary's daughter? Not the people on the ground doing it – but the leader? Because I'm certain the abduction is linked with the stenocryst business...

Claude Chaumet:

I am thinking. *(Pause)* There is no such person within our country. I lead our people there, and I have given you my word, you know what I am trying to do. This is very significant news! *(Pause)* Whoever leads this operation is someone with influence, and knowledge, and who is using my people for – I presume my people – for certain ends. Someone who has got hold of hotheads like this poet...

Ben Maddox:

Has the poet got a name?

Claude Chaumet:

No. *Anonyme.* But he has to be being used, him or another, by someone else. The People's Democratic Party of Magayana does not have such organisation, nor such funds, to get inside a Home Secretary's life.

Ben Maddox:

OK.

Claude Chaumet:

It has to be on the orders of people who want me out and fighting, holding up the processes, for their own ends...

Ben Maddox:

While they search for stenocryst, because if it's in Magayana it's only a matter of time before it's going to be found somewhere else...

Claude Chaumet:

Someone in a country that would be affected badly. America? American CIA? That would be a guess... (*Pause*)

Ben Maddox:

And not a bad one! I wonder?! OK, thanks, Mr Chaumet, I thought you'd like to know. And I'll be in touch if I get any further on this.

Claude Chaumet:

I have a lot to think about.

Ben Maddox:

Sure. Cheers, then. (*Ends – the line goes dead*)

CONFIDENTIAL FILE

Ben Maddox – notes on interview with
Wayne Bowyer, no fixed address : made
Friday 25th October, around noon, Hounslow.

Followed up lead from West Drayton police
station, complaint from Wayne Bowyer – a
homeless young man early twenties – said
he was assaulted inside a lock-up where he'd
taken shelter. Police not very interested
in following up, say the boy's a known drug
user and fantasizer – though they contacted
me because Bowyer claimed to remember
some of a white van number-plate in the
lock-up where he was assaulted.

I'd previously circulated this number-plate
to all local nicks – seen on a vehicle
reported for being parked illegally near
Kensington School last Tuesday week on the
night of Princess Anne's visit.

Found Bowyer selling 'The Big Issue' outside
Safeway in Hounslow. With dog (also
attacked in the lock-up according to
Bowyer).

Bowyer says he found a roller shutter open
at a lock-up nearby and went inside to
shelter from rain, Tuesday evening, 22nd.
A woman returned when he was asleep and

attacked him. She called someone to help
her (he can't remember the name but it
sounded foreign). This other person went
for him, 'gave him a going-over' and
'chucked him out'.

The next day, seeing the dog still in
pain, he complained to the police.

The number-plate was X reg. and
contained the letters KM or FM or FKM.
The false number-plate on the white
Transit van parked near the school was
XOIFKM.

Am noting this prior to (hopefully) being
taken to the lock-up by Bowyer (and his
limping dog!).

STANLEY, PERTH, SCOTLAND

Caitlin Jones kept her mobile telephone line free all the time. Anyone who phoned her on it – apart from Dennis – was given the quick cut. But by the tenth day she wasn't holding things together very well; no word from the people who were holding her daughter; and she felt more strongly than ever that Dennis was wrong. Criminally wrong. It was no good waiting for those terrorists to do what they wanted to do, Dennis *had* to give in over the Chaumet thing. Who cared about political expediency compared with Fran's safety?

She told him so, cried it down the phone, and when he wouldn't give her a direct answer she threw down her mobile in disgust – and then immediately went feeling for it under her sister's sofa. From her briefcase she found her Filofax, looked up a number and tapped it in. The call was answered promptly.

'Leonards.' The voice was business-like but welcoming, with a faint Suffolk accent.

'Johnnie?'

'Who's this?'

'Caitlin Jones – Katey.'

'Katey! Long time! And a long way, girl, congratulations! All those marvellous books, and a cabinet minister husband...' Even old university friends from Footlights days are impressed with a Home Secretary. There would have followed the usual enquiries about each other's families, but Caitlin brought it to the point, because Johnnie Leonard had gone on from Cambridge into Intelligence at MI5 and he now ran a private agency. Like the American Krol, it mainly worked for big insurance companies, the people who received the sort of threats that the Scotts had had.

Within a few minutes of precious mobile phone time – when Dennis might just be coming back with a decision about Chaumet for Fran – Caitlin told her old student revue partner what had happened, laid it all out for him. 'Johnnie, can you help me?' she pleaded. 'Dennis doesn't want Special Branch crawling all over this – well, I wouldn't mind, they're good, but the PM would have to know…'

There was no sucking of teeth at the other end but an immediate reply. 'I'll meet you. Dinner tonight at Rules, their private room.'

'I'm out of London. Scotland…'

'Can you get to Edinburgh?'

'Yes.'

'I'll be on the afternoon flight. Meet me in the Balmoral bar with a large scotch and a good memory for what was in the text message. What about the note they sent? Has Dennis got it?'

'Photocopy. Of a photocopy, but I've got the one they sent; because I thought I might be doing this… But he mustn't know, Johnnie.'

'He won't! We're good at our game, Katey – I'll bring you our brochure!' He laughed, but cut it off quickly. 'We'll help you, Katey, this is our territory. Six o'clock. Can do?'

'Can do.'

And the line, in true Secret Service style, went dead, no signing off. So Johnnie Leonard didn't hear Caitlin suddenly break down and mumble her prayers at the mobile phone that nothing terrible had happened to her daughter yet.

DOWNING STREET SW1

The PM agreed to see Dennis Scott at very short notice. In ten minutes time he had a meeting with the Magayanan

Ambassador who was coming to seek assurances about Claude Chaumet's deportation – so he needed word from the Home Secretary just beforehand that everything was going forward as it should.

But the PM wasn't about to hear what he wanted. Fresh from the entreaties of Caitlin, and with a last check of his silent, message-less mobile phone, Dennis Scott had come to tell the PM what he had been threatened not to tell him. He had come to inform him that his daughter had been kidnapped, that CCTV tape showed it happening.

'My God, Dennis! My God! Are you sure? Are you certain she's not just gone off with a boyfriend…?'

Dennis Scott managed not to tell the PM that he shouldn't judge everyone's actions by his own behaviour. Sitting in the private office on the second floor, he showed him the photocopied note and the text message he'd received. 'This was last week, Alan! These, and one message from her on a recording telling us she was OK. But God knows if she is! God knows what they're doing to her! And the days are running out, they gave me ten days to set Chaumet free…'

'They're doing nothing to her! If they've got any sense.' The PM got to his feet. 'Special Branch, MI5, they know the pattern of these things. And they'll pull out all the stops!' he said. 'Get back to your office and they'll be around by the time you arrive. But nothing must stop our arrangement with Magayana. They'll find her, Dennis, they're marvellous at that sort of thing. Give them the facts and they perform miracles, those boys and girls…'

Scott stood, too. 'If I can just delay the announcement before we say we're deporting the man. I need those precious days up to ten…'

But the PM was adamant. 'Dennis, we don't give in to terrorist threats! Never! Give in on this and the world sees us as a soft option—'

'Does the world have to know?'

'The Magayanan ambassador coming here now wants assurances that we're on the level with his people. I've had President Gomez on the phone again. They can go to any bloody country in the world to flog their stenocryst, that's what they're saying, underneath the polite talk. But we suit them, we're putting up the capital and giving them a good deal, miles better than the Americans would. The Americans would swallow them up, another state star on the spangled flag. But we're making them respectable partners on the world stage. So they play ball with us and we play ball with them...'

Dennis Scott squared to him. 'Even at the cost of my daughter's life? What sort of ball game is that?'

'Nonsense! We'll have her free in no time once I've picked up this phone. They'll be onto every Magayanan national who's ever entered Britain, probably got a tail on some of them right now – because we trust no one, you know that, not since Al Qaeda.. You've done the right thing, believe me...'

'I'm risking everything just telling you...'

'And you should have done it days ago. But remember, we don't give in to terrorism. And I'm telling our Magayanan friend in a minute that you'll announce on Monday.'

Dennis Scott's hands fell to his sides. *'Monday?'*

'Monday. Stay strong, Dennis! OK, Chaumet's appeal is your department, I can't over-ride you except in a State of Emergency, and I won't over-ride you – our politics have to be normally conducted and seen to be so. But we all have to stay strong, together, and I know I can depend on you.' The PM patted Scott on the shoulder. 'Monday. By which time your daughter will be back in the bosom of her family. Trust me.' And with a look out of the window he saw the Magayanan ambassador's car coming into Downing Street; and with very few further words he had Dennis Scott discreetly taken to his car by the back door.

HOUNSLOW, MIDDLESEX

The moment they came in, locking the door behind them, Fran knew that this was what had been coming. Behind their disguises their eyes showed some terrible intent. They came two-handed, but only the woman could look Fran in the face. She was holding the cassette recorder that she had claimed off her ten minutes before.

'What is it? What do you want?' Fran shouted at them, backing away fast at the sight of those eyes.

The woman stood inside the door with her feet apart, holding the recorder in front of her. She looked like a prisoner officer from Holloway, one of those to whom Fran would never have gone for tender loving care. But the man shrugged – and would have shown her his Pontius Pilate hands, she was sure, except he was holding something behind his back like an executioner with the axe.

What? What was it? What were they going to do? Fran screamed, and screamed again, and again. 'What's that?' Her hand shook as she pointed. *'What are you going to do?'* Was it a gun, a knife, a machete? Was this it, was this the time? Was she going to be killed? She screamed again. *'Mum! Mum!'* she shrieked hopelessly.

'Yeah! Yeah! More o' that!' the woman growled – as she clicked on a button of the cassette recorder.

Fran stared at their slitted eyes, her back to the sink. 'I'll give a message! I'll give a message!' she cried. 'Tell me what you want me to say...'

And she screamed again as the man brought his hands round from behind his back – for her to see what was in them. A doubled-over length of thin, spiteful, washing-line rope.

'No! No!' She screamed again, hoarse with screaming. Was he going to hang her? Tie her up and strangle her? She couldn't back off any further, the sink was pressed hard into her spine; she couldn't run, she couldn't hide, she was too far away from the bucket to grab it and use it – so she suddenly did the only thing she could and took a great leap forward, went for him, her black nails tearing at his neckerchief, his eyes. She'd mark him, she'd do him some damage before she was finished! But he skipped back like a boxer, her clawing caught only his shirt – as the woman dropped the recorder onto the table and came for her, a vicious kick into her leg, and a grab round her neck to hold her, hard and hurting.

'Leave the strugglin', girl! I've been beaten! Everyone's been beaten! Jesus before the Holy Cross! Only snotty little English girls don't get beaten!' She yanked at Fran's neck – who was shouting and screaming again and still trying to get at Baptiste – and pulled her off her feet onto the concrete floor. 'You'll suffer what's coming!'

'No! No!'

The man was wrapping the rope round his hand, staring down at Fran, his eyes bulging fit to come out of their sockets. 'I'm so sorry, girl!' he said.

'Stop! No! Stop!' Fran yelled, and screamed again – a long, long scream of desperation and fear. *Don't you touch me!*

The woman grabbed a hard hand at her T-shirt; but before she could get a grip, all at once Fran wasn't the only one shouting. There was a sudden, loud, incoherent yelp like a dog being hurt – as Baptiste fell heavily onto the concrete next to Fran, cracking his head and thrashing his limbs, arching his back, sucking for breath behind his neckerchief. Instantly he was bleeding hard from the head, his body and limbs jerking violently, and there was a pool of wet on the floor as if the bucket had been kicked.

'Sweet Jesus!' the woman shouted. 'Get up! Get up, man!' She let go of Fran to go to his convulsing body, and in panic she tried to still the moving limbs with one hand as she tore off his neckerchief to get at his gasping mouth with the other. 'What's the problem? What you doin', man?'

But Fran knew what he was doing. He was having a fit. He was an epileptic who was out of drug control.

'Let me!' she shouted at the woman. 'It's a fit! A seizure! Let me! I know!' Fran crawled across to the stricken man.

'What? What? What d'you know?' the woman yelled at her, still fierce in the eyes, her hands all over the man and doing no good at all at stopping the thrashing limbs.

'I know what to do!' Fran told her. 'And I'll do it. I'll help you, you help me.'

'What d'you mean?' Still there was no chance of the woman stopping the convulsions, however hard she pressed her weight on his legs.

'You let me go!'

'Let you go? *Let you go?*' The woman was looking around, at Fran, at the door, clearly weighing up her options. Was the man important enough for letting Fran go? 'Yeah! Yeah!' she suddenly said. 'I let you go.'

'Unlock the door then!'

Still the man was twitching and jerking, his head was still bleeding heavily, running into the concrete, and every breath was being fought for. With another look at him, the woman took the keys from her belt and unlocked the cell door. 'Get to him! Get to him!' she shouted, keeping herself on the door side of Fran.

Fran scuttled over to the mattress and snatched up her pillow, lifted the man's head and put it under him. Now she saw his face clearly, a contorted, confused face with eyes wide open but seeing nothing. With the pillow there, she felt at his mouth for any obstacle – chewing gum or false teeth – but finding none she ran over to the sink for water to soak a rag for pressing on his bleeding head.

'Leave the head, girl! Just stop the almighty jerking!'

'The jerking will stop when it's ready – but he'll lose a lot of blood.' She tied his neckerchief around the rag-staunched wound. 'Where's his tablets?' she asked.

'Tablets? What tablets?'

'In the bottle. From the washroom. White, with the Ms on them.'

And the woman flicked her fingers the way the man did, angry with herself. 'Gone. Got none.'

But the convulsions were calming, the man's eyes were rolling, and he started groaning, settled into a deep breathing. And as he did, Fran bent to him and rolled him onto his side in the recovery position she'd been taught to use on Mikey.

'He's going to be all right,' she told the woman. 'But you'll have to get him some more Mysoline. He'll have to see a doctor...'

'Oh, yes?' the woman asked. 'Will he?'

While as calmly, as quietly as she could bring herself to do it, Fran started to walk towards the unlocked door.

But, 'Are you kidding?!' the woman said, suddenly grabbing at Fran and throwing her back across the room, tripping her over the man's unconscious body and landing her on the mattress in a heap.

'That's what you have to do!' Fran shouted up at her. 'Nothing can stop the convulsions! Holding their legs and arms makes them worse...'

'Well, praise to Jesus, he's all right now!' And with a sharp eye on Fran, the woman stooped to pick up the fallen washing line rope, and, checking the cassette recorder with a quick eye, she came to stand menacingly over Fran. 'An' maybe you'll be let to live as a thank you for your help. Meantime, girl, you still got some hollerin' to do for this machine!'

At which Fran screamed her head off as she tried to pull the blanket over herself.

Ben Maddox had walked the industrial estate with Wayne Bowyer and seen just about every unit there. Bowyer's memory was not as good on places as it was on number-plates – but along one fairly deserted, oil-patched concrete road, the old limping dog suddenly started to pull back on its lead. Somehow, he didn't want to go any further in this direction.

'Get on, boy, come on Sid, get on, will yer.' Wayne Bowyer had a plastic knife of a thin white face, weak arms where a bag of *Big Issue's* hung heavy, and altogether wasn't much of a match for a determined dog. He pulled the rope to go on but the dog resisted; and then the fact of where they were began to come to him. 'Could be near 'ere. It's the dog. 'E's like this in the 'ostel, gets a kickin' 'stead of supper there. 'S why I sleep rough...'

Ben looked on down the empty road. 'A roller shutter?' he asked. 'You said it had a roller shutter.'

'Yeah! An' I meant it.' A bit defiant now.

'Well, there's one down there, on the left.'

Wayne Bowyer sharpened his face to look. 'Could be it, that one. Yeah.' But Sid the dog was not prepared to help him to find out; he wasn't going a paw further. 'Yeah, I reckon that's it. An' me an' Sid are out of it.' And he put out his hand for what he'd been promised.

Ben gave him the banknote that had been folded into his palm for a discreet pay-off. 'You reckon, then?'

'Oh, yeah, I reckon.' Wayne Bowyer turned the dog, and without another word was pulled off at a run in the direction from which they'd come.

Ben walked on along what he now saw was Denby Avenue. He had worn trainers today which made no sound, although the planes landing into Heathrow, low enough to count the rivets under their wings, made soft soles superfluous; and with the emptiness of the area right now he could take it slowly, he didn't have to act the busy passer-by. Across the road was a locked, chain-linked compound with a couple of old lorries in it, tarpaulins tied across the windscreens. And on this side, a two-storey brick building with windows upstairs but none below. It had a front door with just a letterbox, and judging by the dust down the cracks, it hadn't been opened in years. Next to it was a roller shuttered entrance wide enough for a small vehicle, and at the far side, an alley, blocked off by a wall, the only feature in which was a dirty, frosted window. This looked like an M.O.T. station, something like that.

It all looked so deserted; the area was probably primed for the development of a new runway at Heathrow. Somewhere further along Ben heard a vehicle revving, but here there was nothing to see: there was no sign of life, all 'shut up and gone away' as his mother would say. He took a note of the grimy numbers on the front door, 36-38, and decided to go back to West Drayton police station to find out what he could about this place. But he'd probably been done for his expenses banknote by Wayne Bowyer and Sid: he was far from convinced that he was where the kid and the dog had got the kickings. What had happened to them could have happened anywhere in Hounslow.

But as he turned away to go back to some sort of civilisation, he suddenly stopped. What was that? What had he heard in a rare moment between the everlasting roar of landing jets? It could have been the keening of a seabird in the distance – but what seabirds flew around here? And then he thought he knew. This the wrong place? No way! He'd found what he was looking for, hadn't he – if that was the sound of a girl screaming...

The screaming repeated, several shrieks in a string, followed by silence. Definitely screaming. Ben's heart quickened; a squirt of adrenalin primed him for action. But what action? There were two things he certainly couldn't do. There was no time in this desolate place to call for the police, ten days she'd been given, according to Scott talking to Chaumet, and this sounded like Day Ten; and there was no knocking on this front door or banging on the shutter. What sort of kidnapper would open up to him – and wouldn't they be tooled up if they did?

But a run to the alley at the side offered a chance. The downstairs window was barred and the top opening to it was far too small to get in through. But on the floor above, in the way upstairs and downstairs plumbing marry up, there was another window, and a soil pipe coming down.

This upstairs window was closed, too, but it had no bars across it.

Could he get in up there? There was just a chance. He tried the soil pipe, but it was shaky, loose into the wall, and he wouldn't get far up that without it crashing down. He knew straight off, though, that the alley was a good width for another way of climbing: the technique where feet are pressed against one side and the back is pressed against the other, up the wall like a mountaineer going up a 'chimney'. And Ben wasn't worried about the height. What he'd discovered when he'd worked in Zippo's Circus was that he was OK high up in the Big Top.

And now, this close, he could hear not screaming but shouting – female voices he thought, but he wasn't waiting to check. He went for it, braced himself between the wall and hitched himself up, and up. Chimneying is a slow climb, but Ben went as fast as he could, no pauses, no checking his height off the ground, no stops for breath, and soon he was level with the top window. And, God bless the architect, the building on the opposite side had a window sited at the same height – which meant there was a narrow sill to perch his backside upon.

From here he looked across at the target window. It was the same design as the one beneath it, frosted glass again with a small aperture at the top – closed. But a good thrust with the soles of his trainers could break the main pane of glass and he could climb in, couldn't he? Which would not be a silent action. He looked up at the slit of sky as an aeroplane went over, low, a DC10, almost drowning the sound of another sudden scream from inside the building, spurring him to go now. But, no, a few seconds' wait might pay off by giving him the shock of surprise. So he waited,

waited, willing the next arrival to come over before any screaming started again: but for a while there was a silence from inside the building – and, thank God, over came a low and heavy jumbo 747. It was so low it shook the window frame and rattled a filling in Ben's teeth, and as it did, Ben clutched at the sill on his side and suddenly kicked out with his feet at the glass of the opposite window.

Crack! Splinter! He nearly lost his grip and fell to the alley below, but a quick push with a foot hard into the wall held him there and he had another go. Smash! Now the pane caved in, and pulling himself back to crouch on his sill, Ben stepped bent double across, took a deep breath, and threw himself head-first into the room – never mind the cuts to his hands and his reefer.

He was in a lavatory with three cubicles and a sink, no urinals, it had to be the office loo for female staff. He picked glass out of his clothing and trod carefully over to the door, pulling at the handle carefully, slowly, to open it.

He was on a small landing with a pile of dusty, unopened mail and old directories with a broken telephone slung on top. The stairs were concrete – and just as he was feeling pleased about that, no creaking as he went down, there came another loud scream from downstairs. A girl! Definitely a girl!

He didn't wait now. He took the stairs like falling, came to a corridor at the bottom and turned to his left. There were two doors here, one on each side of the corridor. The door on the left was ajar and opened into a kitchen, which was empty. So whoever was screaming had to be in the other one.

And now he wished he'd come better prepared, and with police back-up. A weapon would have been good! But what was a kitchen for, if it didn't have knives? Quickly, still silently, Ben stepped back into the kitchen – and gently tried the drawers for what he wanted. But as he was rooting, taking out a 'kitchen devil' knife, he saw something better. There, across the room, lying on a cluttered work surface was a blade – a machete; the sort he'd seen the sugar cutters carrying in Petit Fleuve, just a bit shorter but long enough.

He grabbed the weapon. So – whoever was in that other room didn't have this! He came back to the other door, didn't know whether or not it would be locked, but he had to assume that it wasn't because he wasn't going to knock! He backed off across the corridor, into the other opening, then suddenly spurted forward, hand on the door handle, twisted it, and burst into the other room.

To be confronted by a body on the floor, a girl being held round the mouth by a big woman in a cotton balaclava who was levelling something at him. A gun. A black automatic.

'Ground that! Put that down!' the woman shouted at him. She shook the automatic to add to the command, but it was her eyes that told him she would use it.

Ben didn't take his eyes off the gun as he laid the machete onto the floor. Stooping gave time, and he was less of a target. And, bending nearer, a quick glance down at the body on the floor told him that this was his photo-fit from the CCTV, and he wasn't dead but breathing, starting to groan with the eyelids fluttering.

And the girl was almost certainly Fran Scott.

'You can get out of this!' he told the woman, coming up slowly. 'Let the girl go – and I'll let you go.'

The woman made a weird sneering sound behind her balaclava. 'You're not stationed to let anyone go. Get over 'gainst that wall!'

Ben moved backwards, slowly. Still keeping the gun pointed at his chest, the woman reached forward with her foot and drew the machete towards her across the concrete floor. She was tall, strongly built – and in command. 'I got a job to do!' she said. 'And you can see it and hear it since you're here. See what screamin' and hollerin' the cut of a blade can raise!'

'You'll shoot me first!' Ben said.

'Then or after, it's all the same at this stage o' things!' The woman suddenly let go the hand round Fran's mouth, grabbed at the machete, and in one swift sugar cutter's movement, raised it to slash at Fran's arm as if it were cane.

But it didn't land – it dropped: because the figure on the floor had suddenly grabbed hold of the cassette recorder and thrown it at the woman, hitting her on the blade hand. *'No!'* the man shouted. 'Don't you cut the girl!'

He hadn't seen Ben yet, and Ben suddenly jumped. He leapt across and grabbed the wavering gun off the woman – and he was at her chest with it, his own hostage.

'I'll use it!' he shouted. *'I'll use it!'*

Fran was on her feet.

'Get that rope! Tie her hands!' Ben shouted at her. He backed off to stoop and hold the kitchen devil from up his sleeve at the man's throat. 'I'll use this, too!' he threatened.

And within twenty seconds the power in the room had changed. It was the woman who was hobbled with the rope, inside a cell that was locked from the outside, the man locked in the washroom, while Ben reached for his mobile phone.

'My dad!' Fran said. 'My dad first!' And she rattled off his mobile number, before calmly, unbelievably calmly, walking into her captors' kitchen and rooting into the fridge for a 'coca' – before she collapsed, crying in shock on the floor.

WELL DONE BEN!

THE ZEPHON

NEWSROOM'S PROUD

OF ITS NEW SON!

Working with
you, I like!
        Jonny

Leave space for
me on your
assignments
    Bloom
XXXXXXXXXX

Break a leg on the night —
    Spiderman! The team.

Ben had all the congratulations a proud newsroom gives to one of its own who has been brave and professional – and some of them meant it. But Ben wasn't surfing on this wave of praise; because at Hounslow he'd been forced to do things that he wished he hadn't. He told Kath Lewis, 'I *had* to phone the police. The woman was bleeding and still looked dangerous; if she'd come for me I'd have had to shoot her; the man was bleeding from the head; and Fran Scott, the poor kid, was in shock. So there was no way I could make her safe and sit on two kidnappers for a few days to force Scott's hand...'

Kath slapped her desk. 'Maddox, we report the news; OK, we ask all the awkward questions to keep the public informed, and we investigate things people don't know about, they're our jobs – but when we're *making* the news we're no longer doing that job. That's for documentary makers. In News we have to look impartial even if we're not – and you remember that, next time you're James Bonding around.'

Ben said nothing; he couldn't trust himself to keep his remarks professional.

'Now,' Kath went on, flourishing Ben's note that was in her hand, the memo telling her that he'd got everything together for a 'World View' special, 'we've scheduled this for Monday night, prime time. Your file looks good – so get the script written and I'll have it by Sunday at noon. That just about gives us time to get all the visual packages in place, the graphics done and the permissions in the bag.'

But Ben still looked unhappy. 'You did a day's work,' Kath told him, 'for which you're paid, so smile! Let someone else rule the world. And when you put in your expenses make them reasonable. If anyone's a hero in my books it's in my accounts books…'

'I ruined a good reefer jacket,' Ben said.

'*A reefer jacket,* he says! I'll find you a raincoat of Len's!' She waved a smoothing hand at him. 'But you can bump things up a bit.'

Ben shook his head at her, his thoughts still on that other agenda. 'Kath, I went home with the daughter in the police car, I had half an hour with Scott and I told him all the Magayanan stuff, I tried to sell him Chaumet's line – and so did she, the girl, when she realised the kidnappers' demands. But they're stubborn mules, politicians: polite, but stubborn – and while I reckon he'll always do me a few press favours, it's never going to affect his politics. Public School and Cambridge – you don't change old boy loyalties, not even for daughters…' And with that Ben huffed out, to start a hard thirty-six hours work on the script he had to write for the following Monday night's programme.

But, unknown at that moment to Ben, three things were happening. One was the ordering by Kath Lewis of a case of Merlot to be delivered to Ben's Hackney flat. The second was a telephone call from Dennis Scott inviting him and Meera to dinner at Kensington Mews on the following Monday evening – which Ben would have to decline for 'World View'. And the third was a press release by the PM. Which read:

FROM THE OFFICE OF
THE PRIME MINISTER

For immediate release

Today two Magayanan terrorists have been arrested following a secret kidnap operation involving a member of a cabinet minister's family. Her Majesty's government is happy and relieved to report that the kidnap victim, about whom more details will be released later, is safe and reunited with family members.

This was a high level kidnapping intended to influence the government's decision making.

Although a decision has been reached, it has been for this reason that no announcement has been made in the past few days by the Right Honourable Dennis Scott, MP, on the matter of the deportation appeal received from Claude Chaumet, the Opposition Leader of Magayana. It can now be announced that this decision will be reported to parliament during parliamentary business at twelve noon in the House of Commons on Monday next, 28th October.

Press statement ends.

Press Office, 10 Downing Street SW1.

Which – when Bloom phoned it through to him – Ben knew meant that the Magayanan plot had finally failed. Rescuing Fran Scott had helped not only her, it had dug the government out of a deep hole. By the time he presented his 'World View' special, Claude Chaumet would be on his way to Magayana.

WESTMINSTER SW1

There was only a typical Monday morning attendance in the Commons for the Chaumet statement to be made by the Home Secretary. Most MPs went to their constituencies over the weekend, and it took more than a routine, well-trailed announcement by the Home Secretary to get them back from a long weekend before lunchtime; but the London based members made up a smattering of an audience for the expected declaration by the Right Honourable Dennis Scott – although none of them had guessed his connection with the recent kidnapping.

The PM was still being driven back from Chequers so did not attend, although Ben Maddox was outside on Parliament Green with Jonny and a sound girl. He had broken off from studio rehearsals to cover the announcement so that Zephon had one consistent face to front their Magayana coverage. Win or lose over Chaumet, they had to report the news; and what Ben knew from brother Pat was that within two hours of the Commons announcement the Home Office would have Chaumet down at Gatwick and on the next flight out to Magayana, which was being covered by another Zephon team led by Bloom.

As an October gust blew in off the Thames, Ben shivered in his suit on Parliament Green, his reefer jacket too tattered and torn to be seen on TV. And he shivered inside, knowing that however often a live reporting journalist does it, cold fingers of fear grip the gut as the countdown to a cue comes into the earpiece.

KENSINGTON MEWS W8

For Fran – apart from relating details of her ordeal – there had been no talking to Dennis Scott. There had been kissing, hugging, rejoicing when the Edinburgh train got in – but the Home Secretary within his own four walls was not going to discuss the politics of the Chaumet affair. Family was family, love was love, but the terrorists were locked up in Belmarsh prison and all the Scotts were safe. Now it was back to work full time, and no one was allowed to interfere in Scott's government business, especially when he had a crucial statement to make in the House that was so essential to the Prime Minister and the party.

Fran was in a weird state. She was safe, she had clean

clothes, she had her own bathroom again and she slept in her own sweet sheets. She had had a laugh on the phone with Gussie, and she could speak openly to real people instead of secretly into a cassette recorder. She ate the food she liked, she went to the kitchen when she wanted and helped herself to whatever hot or cold drinks she fancied, and she rejoiced in the dear sounds of Mikey's and her parents' voices.

But she was still upset by something; by someone; and that was the man, Baptiste. She had told her father, cried to her father, that Baptiste had saved her from injury – and he had still waved it away. He had shown no emotion over that fact that the man had had an epileptic fit at the thought of hurting her; that in the end the terrorist was on her side. Baptiste had stopped the woman from making a recording of her screaming that her father would have wept to hear. In reality, he had saved her as much as Ben Maddox had, and Ben Maddox was declared a hero. But none of that made any difference to Dennis Scott. All she got from her father was, 'He'll have a trial. What comes out then will come out then. Meanwhile I have my job to do.'

All the same, Fran watched the parliamentary coverage of her father, choosing the Zephon Television channel, of course. Ben Maddox had told her that any Chaumet-related stuff would have him involved – and she had to watch him, didn't she?

Allowed a day off school until after Chaumet had been sent back, she switched on to Zephon News. And she watched with her knuckles in her mouth as Ben, in a smart suit, did his stuff from 'on the road' outside parliament. In the darkness of those awful nights, watching television was something she had thought that she would never do again...

ZEPHON TELEVISION

Transcript for Legal Department

PROGRAMME: ZT/N/30/10   **LIVE NEWS**

TRANSMISSION: 12.05 30/10

PARLIAMENTARY COVERAGE – O/B AND INT.
CHAMBER, HOUSE OF COMMONS

Ben Maddox:

(To camera, Parliament Square) In a few moments we're going
to hear from Dennis Scott. He's expected to announce the
failure of Claude Chaumet's appeal against his deportation
to Magayana, where he is the official opposition leader.
For those new to it, the background to the case is
complicated— *(Interruption, Ben puts hand to earpiece)* But
I'm hearing we have pictures from inside the Commons
now where Dennis Scott, the Home Secretary is already
on his feet. Let's go directly into the Commons...

Rt. Hon Dennis Scott:

*(At the Dispatch Box inside the House of Commons – pictures from
Parliamentary TV)* Mr Speaker, I have come to the House
today to announce my decision regarding the appeal
against deportation lodged by Mr Claude Chaumet, the
leader of the People's Democratic Party of Magayana,
which honourable friends will know is the official
Opposition to the ruling party of President Jorge Gomez.
Mr Chaumet was charged under English law with offences
relating to the United Kingdom's residency rules for
foreign politicians and activists and was found guilty of

transgressing them. The details of these charges, Mr Speaker, and of the judge's decision are in the Library of the House. I have now carefully considered Mr Chaumet's appeal against the guilty finding and his further appeal against deportation to Magayana. The House will come to know that I have been under considerable personal pressure from Magayanan sources – not, I am assured, connected with Mr Chaumet – to allow the appeal, to let him stay to continue his campaign. *(Dennis Scott drinks water from the glass on the table)* That personal pressure is no longer upon me. *(Drinks again)* As Her Majesty's Home Secretary charged with a duty to decide such an appeal, and as one whose decision, this way or that, is binding upon the government, I have come to the conclusion that Mr Chaumet's appeal should be allowed. Mr Chaumet will not be deported. *(The House erupts with noise. Government front and back-benchers stand, wave Order Papers and shout at Scott. Those Opposition members present point at the government benches and jeer. Members from outside begin hurrying into the Chamber)*

Mr Speaker:

(Standing) Order! Order! The Right Honourable Member will be heard! Order! *(Sits)*

Dennis Scott:

(Resuming his feet) My reasons for this decision are outlined in a written statement that I have also placed in the Library. *(In a shout to counter continuing jeers and catcalls)* I will tell you this. I have listened to opinions both official and close to home, although they might

have thought that those entreaties fell on deaf ears at the time. But the truth of it is, as I faced the possibility of the execution of one dear to me, that I cannot risk the same happening to any man of good faith. I believe that justice will not be served by deporting a man who is representing the interests of his people against an oppressive regime. Unlike our Home Office credo, Magayana is not a "safe, just and tolerant society" – not for many of its people, and not for those who oppose its government. I have understood better recently how politically and tribally divided that country is, and in my opinion, on greater reflection, the sugar growing people of Magayana deserve to share in any mineral wealth that the country owns. To this end, I have written over the weekend to the Secretary General of the United Nations recommending that a UN inspection team be sent to Magayana with the purpose of reporting on matters of human rights in that country. *(Further shouts from Members and admonishments from Mr Speaker)*

Dennis Scott:

(Continuing) Furthermore, I am embarrassed that my personal opinion is now at odds with the official view of Her Majesty's government, and having come late to holding that view, I feel it right and proper now to resign my position as Her Majesty's Secretary of State for Home Affairs, a post that I have been proud to hold. Mr Speaker, I depart with immediate effect. *(Shouts, jeers and counter-cheers)* This decision has been communicated to the Prime Minister by telephone. I have nothing further to add to the House and will make

no further statement for the moment outside this place.

(Dennis Scott drinks again, sits, to uproar, gathers his papers, stands, and with a bow to the Speaker, exits the Commons)

(Cut to Ben Maddox at Parliament Green)

<u>Ben Maddox:</u>

Well, you heard it! Dennis Scott has resigned as Home Secretary and Claude Chaumet is free to pursue his campaign from Britain on behalf of his people in Magayana. Also, the United Nations has been asked to investigate human rights issues in Magayana – an issue we will be looking at in 'World View' on Zephon Television this evening. *(Looking around)* Reactions here will follow as and when a stunned House of Commons comes out to talk to us on Parliament Green. Meanwhile, from Westminster this is Ben Maddox handing you back to the studio.

(OB ends)

KENSINGTON MEWS W8

Fran Scott couldn't believe what she had just seen and heard. Her father had changed his mind! He'd given no hint of heeding what she or Ben Maddox had said, but all the time their words must have been feeding deep into his sense of decency, together with his realisation of the human results that political decisions could have. When he'd gone over and over the appeal papers, and when he'd thought and thought about what martyrdom meant – where it wasn't so much about sainthood as blood on the floor – the rights of what those Magayanans were fighting for had got through to him. And, of course, it had to:

or how could he possibly still be married to Caitlin Jones with all the human rights she stood up for?

And brill for him! Except, he could have said…

Fran jumped up as her mother came into the room behind her. She had been watching the broadcast in her study, and she was crying.

'I'm proud of him!' Caitlin said. 'Underneath, he's a very decent man…'

They hugged, hard and long, part of the hug still for the recent past, and part a hug for today.

Fran pulled away. 'Good old Dad! I might even vote for him one day! And I was wrong about something myself,' she added.

'Yes?'

Fran hung her head, then looked up at her mother and smiled. 'When he finished that speech, he bowed to Mr Speaker – out of his respect for our democracy, where he can do the sort of thing he's done. Which those Magayanans haven't got. So what I'm saying is – perhaps it wouldn't always be wrong to curtsey, not if you really respect someone…'

'Perhaps not.'

'Williams at school might have been right. And when Dad comes in through that door, I'm going to give him a millimetre, only a token millimetre, mind, of a curtsey. But you don't tell Gussie!'

'As if! Nor Princess Anne,' Caitlin Jones smiled, 'if ever I get to write her biography…' The telephone suddenly rang and she crossed the room to answer it. 'Here we go!' she said. 'The first of many!'

'No problem! Fielding calls is easy,' Fran said. 'Just tell everyone to watch Ben Maddox tonight!'

DAILY POST
TUESDAY 29 OCTOBER

LAST NIGHT'S TV
WORLD VIEW✶✶✶✶✳

Remember Ben Maddox, the young sprog of Zephon Television who was given a going over by Dennis Scott when he was Home Secretary?

Well, he's grown up! On a 'World View' special last night he presented a dramatic account of a kidnap foiled in part by himself. The victim – as you will see from the front page – was none other than the daughter of Dennis Scott, the man who rubbished him.

In this 60 minute special, we also had a highly watchable account of what is really going on in Magayana, and some of our own prime minister's shenanigans to rule the electronics world. And who was Maddox's special guest? None other than Claude Chaumet, the campaigner for freedom for the oppressed people of his country, just released from house arrest.

This was riveting stuff – presented with clarity and charm by a journalist whose face and voice we are going to watch and trust in times to come.

Well done, Zephon, well done, Maddox! A player in the game, it came over as clear as crystal that not only Scott's daughter but Maddox himself influenced a brave politician's decision to have no truck with dodgy foreign states.

What's your next assignment, Ben? We look forward to seeing it...

© jillyprime@dailypost.co.uk

More Ben Maddox assignments and other fantastic books by Bernard Ashley

BERNARD ASHLEY

£4.99

978 1 84362 204 8

Hard Stew always gets what he wants,
and he wants Davey's new bike.

But Hard Stew's not the only thing bothering
Davey, there's also the big family secret,
the one that everyone wants to keep from him.
A secret more frightening than a hundred Hard Stews.

The sort you've got to stare in the face.
If you've got the guts...

**Shortlisted for the Sheffield Children's Book Award and
the Angus Award**

*'Bernard Ashley's great gift is to turn what seems
to be low-key realism into something much stronger
and more resonant.'*
Philip Pullman

BERNARD ASHLEY

£4.99

978 1 86039 879 7

When Kaninda survives a brutal attack on his village in East Africa, he joins the rebel army, where he's trained to carry weapons, and use them.

But aid workers take him to London where he fetches up in a comprehensive school. Clan and tribal conflicts are everywhere, and on the streets it's estate versus estate, urban tribe against urban tribe.

All Kaninda wants is to get back to his own war and take revenge on his enemies. But together with Laura Rose, the daughter of his new family, he is drawn into a dangerous local conflict that is spiralling out of control.

Shortlisted for the Carnegie Medal and the *Guardian* Children's Fiction Award

'So pacy that it is difficult to turn the pages fast enough.'
The School Librarian

'A gripping and compassionate tale.'
TES

BERNARD ASHLEY

£4.99

978 1 84121 306 4

'Hold on tight!' Tom shouted at the girl. 'Grab hold of the side!'

Tom Welton's never done anything in his life that he's been proud of...really proud of. But a chance rescue of a girl off the Suffolk coast seems to offer him the opportunity to change all that, and soon Tom finds himself risking everything to save her.

GILL LOBEL

£4.99

978 1 84362 448 6

Hazel Anne Mooney: Smart. Funny. Fed up. She's unhappy at school, she's far from model-girl slim, and she's being bullied. Lauren Stevenson: Gorgeous. Glamorous. Texting queen. She's pencil-thin, she's perfect. And she's a bully.

A funny and touching story about teenage girls. Perfect to get your teeth into.

'This is Gillian Lobel's first novel for teenagers and she has a funny appealing style that is bang up-to-date. This book will appeal immediately to all Jacqueline Wilson fans!'
The Bookseller

MORE ORCHARD BLACK APPLES

Down to the Wire	Bernard Ashley	978 1 84616 965 6
Flashpoint	Bernard Ashley	978 1 84616 060 8
Little Soldier	Bernard Ashley	978 1 86039 879 7
Tiger without Teeth	Bernard Ashley	978 1 84362 204 8
Revenge House	Bernard Ashley	978 1 84121 814 4
Freedom Flight	Bernard Ashley	978 1 84121 306 4
Ella Mental and the Good Sense Guide	Amber Deckers	978 1 84362 727 2
A Crack in the Line	Michael Lawrence	978 1 84616 283 1
Hazel, Not a Nut	Gill Lobel	978 1 84362 448 6
The Ghost of Sadie Kimber	Pat Moon	978 1 84362 202 4
Nathan's Switch	Pat Moon	978 1 84362 203 1
Milkweed	Jerry Spinelli	978 1 84362 485 1
Stargirl	Jerry Spinelli	978 1 84616 600 6

All priced at £4.99 or £5.99

Orchard Black Apples are available from all good bookshops,
or can be ordered direct from the publisher:
Orchard Books, PO BOX 29, Douglas IM99 1BQ
Credit card orders please telephone 01624 836000
or fax 01624 837033 or visit our website: www.orchardbooks.co.uk
or e-mail: bookshop@enterprise.net for details.

To order please quote title, author and ISBN
and your full name and address.
Cheques and postal orders should be made payable to 'Bookpost plc.'
Postage and packing is FREE within the UK
(overseas customers should add £1.00 per book).

Prices and availability are subject to change.